MUSASHINO

The Collected Poems of
Toshiaki An
In English & Japanese
Translated by Noriko Mizusaki

安 俊暉 英日詩集

武蔵野

水崎野里子 訳

コールサック社

A Collected Poems of Toshiaki An in English and Japanese

MUSASHINO

Translated by Noriko Mizusaki

安 俊暉 英日詩集

武蔵野

水崎野里子 訳

Contents

目次

Musashino*

*Now Japanese people call the rather larger area around Musashino-shi, in Tokyo, as Musashino. The poet once lived in Musashi-no, in Tokyo. And, he read a book on the cultural exchanges between the ancient Korea and ancient Japan, to suppose that the Japanese present pronounciation, mu-sa-shi-no, was originally pronounced as mao-sa-shi-no: 苧種子 野. 苧 was pronounced as wo, mao, or karamusi, in Japanese. It is a kind of grass to take the fibers and weave linen cloths. In the ancient ages when Korean people immigrated to Japan, they might have brought the seeds to plant the grass in the place in Japan. So it is called Mu(ao) sashi-no. "No" means a field.

Chapter1 Musashino

一章　武蔵野

In Musashino	武蔵野に
Around the time when	桑の実なる頃
Mulberries ripen	君に
I met	出会えり
You	

In Musashino	武蔵野の
Oak leaf turned red	楢紅葉
Each leaf is	一葉は
The sign	君と僕の
Of you and me	しるし

You and me	君と僕
Collecting leaves	武蔵野に
Dyed into the color	染まりゆく
So cherished	木の葉
	大切に
	集むるは

Constantly	絶えず
I return	自己本来に
To myself	たち帰り
My true self	居る

Each time	その都度
When time ripens	時熟し
I talk	独り言のように
Just to myself	語る
By your side	君がそば
I walk home	歩いて帰る
Sensing a vine	かずら手折り
I picked up	香ぎつつ
You	君
A natural beauty	天然の美
Fading away I am	移ろいゆく
You overwhelm	我を
Me	圧倒す
You	君
A girl	少女
Your glance	一瞬の視線
Instantly shot me	我を射る

Your beauty	君が美
Gifted by God	神より来たる
Together with	罪咎
Sins and blames	ともに

When	君
You	故郷
Leave me	茅野に^{*1}
For Chino*1	発つ時
Your hometown	上水べり^{*2}
On a shore of	桑の実
The stream*2	揺る
Mulberries	
Sway	

*1. A city in Nagano.
*2. Tamagawa Water Supply Route at Mitaka. It looks like a stream or brook.

*1　長野にある地名

*2　三鷹にある玉川上水

When	咳込みて
I coughing	君が
Your quince	カリン
I wanted	求めけり

You	君十九
Nineteen years old	時
Time tensed	張りつめる

Your eyes	君が目線
Young though	幼きと
Womanly	女と
Extremely tensed	感極まりて
You removed	イヤリング
Your earrings	外す
So dear	君いとし
Your	君が
Quince	カリン
Before me	わが前に
Fragrant	芳香す
When	君
You	故郷
Leave	茅野に
For Chino	発つ
Your hometown	時

You	君
Young	幼き
Into light pink	うす紅に
A vein	静脈の
Oozing	一すじ
Under skin	滲みをり
You	君
A miracle	奇跡の
The gift	賜もの
On the breast	君が胸に
A vein under the skin	一すじの
Oozing in light pink	静脈
I see	滲みをるも
Rain smokes	雨けむる
A green signal	青信号
On and off	点滅し
And again	また
Into red	赤
You and me	君と僕
Shall part again	またいづれ
Someday	離れゆく

New	新しき
Quince juice	君が
You prescribed	カリン液
Before me	わが前に
Clear	澄めり

You are nineteen	君十九
The last teardrop	十代の
In your teen ages	最後の涙
Goes	我に触れ
Touching me	ゆく

Your brow	君が額
Pale white	仄白き
Your immaturity	未熟ゆえに
Caught	我を
Me	とらえる

At Mitaka	君
Beside the clear stream	三鷹
You	上水べり
Sway	桑の実と
With	共に
Mulberries	揺る

Rain smoky	雨けむる
In it	なか
Time of life	人生の時間
Restless	休みなく
Passing away	過ぎゆく

Mulberries	桑の実
Leaves' shadow	葉影
Dim	淡く
Sways	揺る、奥
At the depths	椋鳥の
A starling I found	一羽あり

Today	今日
I am seeing	君に
You	会う日
Leaves of cherry trees	桜葉に
Songs of a bulbul bird	ひよ鳥の声
Echoes clear	冴ゆ

Last evening	昨夜
I met you	君に会いて
This morning	今朝
A bulbul sings	ひよ鳥の鳴くも
Leaves of cherry trees	桜木の葉影
The shadow	静まりて
Calm	あり

In Musashino	わが
Sometimes	最期かと
I happen to think	思う時
Of my last day	武蔵野にあり
These days	この頃は
Only bulbuls	ひよ鳥のみぞ
Singing	鳴きをりて

Like breezes	君に
That blow	向けて
Towards you	吹く
Like ripples	微風のごと
That approach	君に
Toward you	向けて
Wishing no traces	寄る
To be left	さざ波のごと
In my hesitation	その跡
My being ashamed	留めぬように
For you	はじらいつ
A young lady	ためらいつ
Nineteen years old	十九の君に

You	君
A young girl	少女
Wearing a hat	つば広き
Broad-brimmed	帽子
You gaze	目線に
Something distant	遠きもの
	ありて

You gazing	水平線に
The horizon	凝らす
On the depths	目の奥
Of your eyes	限りなく青く
Infinitely blue	

14

In my childhood	わが
Blossoms of silk trees	幼き頃に
Bloomed	咲きをりし
Now	合歓の花
They bloom out	今
Above you	君が上に
	咲く

The west sun	西日さす
Comes on	わが影
My shadow	何故に
Why now	君に
Overlapping	重なる
With you?	

Reeds	古里の
In my hometown	葦の葉
Sway hastily	急ぎ揺る
Just like	われ
I sway	君に会いてのち
Since I met you	揺るごと

Since	君に会いて
I met you	のちより
The reeds	古里の
In my hometown	葦の葉
Sway in a hurry	急ぎ揺る

In Musashino	武蔵野に
The moon slanting	月傾きて
This evening	今宵
You stay in Chino	君
At the end of	茅野の人
Your nineteen-year-old	十九の終わり
The moon sways	月揺る、

I wake up to hear	目覚むれば
A bulbul bird twitters	ひよ鳥の声
Since	君に会いて
I met you	のちより
Why	何故に
Do I hurry up	生死を急ぐ
Life and death?	浅き夢の中
In a shallow dream	またしても
Repeatedly	遺書を
I am writing	したため
My will	居りぬ

Your	君が
Heart beating and	胸の鼓動と
My beating	わが鼓動
Resound somehow	いづれとも知れず
Overlapping	重なりて鳴る

Keeping neat	整然としていて
Being untidy	雑然としていて
Live oak's lodge	樫の宿
Peaceful	安らぎてあり

On a towel	君が
Remaining	香りありて
Your smell	我も拭く
I wipe myself	タオル
With it	

Screened with	運命の
A thin membrane	薄き膜に
Of destiny	仕切られて
Today	今日
Infinitely	限りなく
Close we are	近くいる

Just like in my hometown	古里に
Pine trees rustle in the wind	松風鳴るごと
Constantly	絶えず
You rustle	君鳴る
Just like a white lily sways	白百合揺るごと
Constantly	絶えず
You sway	君揺る

Violets	すみれ
Dark and light	濃く淡く
Dying each other	染め合いて
Sway	揺る
You and me	君と僕
In a feast on the earth	地上の宴
Shining	オレンジ色に
In orange	輝いて
Again go up	また
Into the heaven	天上となる
In my mind	わが胸に
Constantly rings	絶えず鳴る
Mind of Poetry	詩心
Blowing to pass over	君に
To you	吹き渡りて
Rings	松風のごと
Like a pine wind	鳴る
You and me	君と僕
Tumble down	転倒す
Finding out	あらゆる価値
All the values	再び
Afresh	見出しつつ

We fall in a craze	人は狂い
We then	人は
Awaken	目覚める
Pine winds	松風
Rustle	鳴る
In my hometown	古里
Bunting birds	頬白
Twitter	さえずる
Pine winds	松風
Rustle	鳴る
In undergrowth	下草に
Bellflowers	桔梗
Sway	揺る
Come running	走り来る
You	君
Young	幼く
Breasts	いたく
Ample	胸
Fully	豊か

You rearranged   君
Into a bottle   生け替えし
A gardenia   くちなしの花
With so many leaves   初夏の葉
In the early summer   ふんだんに

Time   君と僕の
For you and me   時
Turns up in the heaven   天上となり
Turns down on ground   地上となり

My destiny   運命の
Permits some to me   許すものと
Not does some to me   許さぬ
                             ものと

Chapter2　Live Oak's Lodge

二章　樫の宿

The day	君に
When I see you	会う日
Now into a distant	遠くして
Again	また
A bulbul bird	ひよ鳥
Afar off	遠く
A cry	鳴く

When I have not	会わないで
Seen you for days	いれば
Even now	すぐ
I want to see	会いたくなる
You	君

This morning	今朝は
Shrikes cry	百舌鳴いて
The time	君と僕の
For you and me	時
Ends	終わる

A mid-autumn	中秋の
Harvest moon	名月
Again	また
It starts to wane	欠けてゆく

In the setteng sun	晩秋の
In the late autumn	夕日のなかに
You and me	君と僕
A tulip tree's	ユリの木の
Each leaf shape	それぞれの
Searched for	葉形
	探しけり
In the late autumn	晩秋の
A tulip tree	ユリの木の
The leaf's shape	葉形
Each by each	それぞれに
You and me	君と僕
You nineteen	君十九
Twenty	二十
Twenty one	二十一と
Like stars	星のごと
Setting	我が位置
My position	定めゆく
You are not	君をらぬ
In the room	部屋
I have been here	我居りて
Feeling like	また
You with me	君をる
Again	気配

23

With me	我に
You here	君をる
I feel like	気配

After	君
You	去りて
Parted from me	のちの
The sorrow	哀愁
Happen to like	ふと好む
I do for myself	我となり

A child of man	人の子
Yoko	容子
You	君
At the age of twenty	二十
On the day	その日
You were	我と過ごし
With me	ゆく

On a twig	樫の枝に
Of the live oak tree	ひよ鳥
A bulbul bird	来鳴きて
Came to sing	樫の宿
In the live oak's lodge	君と僕
You and me	落ち着きぬ
Settled down	

Fragrant olive blossoms	金木犀
Beyond another shore	善悪の
of right and wrong	彼岸
Scenting	香りをり
A bulbul bird	ひよ鳥
Sings	鳴いて
Summer grass	夏草
Swaying	揺るゝ
At the live oak's lodge	樫の宿
Where	君と僕
For you and me	過去現在
The past	未来と
The present	接する
And the future	ところ
Adjoin together	
You	君
Not here	をらぬ
Violets	すみれ
Withered	しおれをり
Only their centers	花芯のみは
Sucked up water	水上げつ

In Musashino	武蔵野の
Oaks and live oaks	楢と樫
Any tree	いづれも
Produces acorns?	どんぐり
You ask to me	なる木かと
Always	問う君
Innocent	いつも
	幼くて

You	君
Put flowers of	生けし花
Mountain burdock	山ごぼうと
And violet	すみれ
In a tiny	小ビンの
Glass bottle	中に

You	君
Put	生けし
Wild crysanthemum	野菊
Flowers	小ビンの中に
In a tiny bottle	また
Also	小さく
Tiny	

Bitter melons	ニガウリの
The yellow flower	黄の花
Hidden	秘めたる
Green I notice	緑注す

In the oak lodge	樫の宿
You and me	君と僕
Taking up the Bible	聖書取りて
Read it	読む

Your nurse cup	ナースキャップ
Innocent	いとけなき
Red cross	赤十字
Beside the window	窓辺
A Himalayan cedar	ヒマラヤ杉

God	神は
Gives	与え
Takes away	奪い
And gives	与える

God	神
Through you	君を通し
Shows me	再び
All of my life	全てを
Again	見せんとす
I live my life	人生を
Two times	二度生きる
With many blames	罪も多き
A red cross	ナースキャップ
On your nurse cap	赤十字の
Thundering rain	君
Falling over	降り包む
On the window	雷雨
You	窓辺
Young	いとけなき
Like green acorns	青どんぐりの
Red cross	赤十字
A pity	灯しをる哀し
You light it up	我昔君と同じ頃
Once	十字架に仕えんと
At the same age with you	志し時あり
I wanted to serve the cross	思いつ
That I was thinking of	

You	君
Not here	をらぬ
Sad is the red cross	赤十字淋しかり
Only summer cicadas	夏蟬のみぞ
Singing loud	鳴きをりて
The Himalayan cedar	ヒマラヤ杉
Sheds leaves	葉散り
Over the ground	敷き

God	神は
For the sake of giving	与えるがゆえに
Gives	与え
For the sake of not giving	与えぬがゆえに
Not to give	与えぬ

Yesterday	昨日
I saw with you	君と見し
Apricot	杏
Today	今日風に
Blown by winds	吹かれをり

This evening	今宵
My choice was	選択は
Just right?	正しきか
On my way back	帰り道
A faint	わずか
Mist	霧
Your house	君が家
When I left	出れば
Misty	霧
I walk	我
With my	わが影と
Shadow	歩めり
You	早春の
In the early spring	君
When I think	思えば
Apricot I see	杏
Apricot flowers	杏花
White	白き
Light red	うす紅の

Your breaths	君が息
Some time when	どこからか
Turn into	寝息と
Sleeping breaths	なるとき

So innocent	無垢なる
Your sleeping breaths	君が寝息
Outside	外
A wind rush	一陣の風
Though a crow	烏
Cawing	鳴くも

The sky	空と
Clouds	雲と
And my position	我の位置

In the evening	夕暮れに
Railways	線路
Parted	別れゆく
A signal	信号
Green	青
Again	また
Red	赤

Daffodil	水仙と
Hyacinth	風信子
Both of them	すべて
My favorite	僕の好きな
Names	名の
Transient	一時のもの

Hyacinth	風信子
My favorite	僕の好きな
Name	名の
Short-lived	はかなく
I wish	開きゆかぬを
It not to open	願う

In Musashino	武蔵野の
Red cross	赤十字
In the sun leaks though trees	秋木洩れ日の
In the autumn	ひよ鳥
A bulbul bird	我呼び
Calls me	鳴く
Sings	

Today	今日
A yellow daffodil	黄水仙
A bit	やゝ
Slanting	はす向きの
What is it	何をか
Thinking?	思わん
In the early spring	早春の
A tulip red	チューリップ
Yellow inside	なか黄
Red again on bottom	その奥また赤の
In the early spring	早春の
A tulip	チューリップ
Beside the window	窓辺
While a young couple	若きカップル
Goes passing	通りすぎる
	間の
Today	今日
Adonis flowers bloom	福寿草
Only around them	そこだけは
Warm	暖かく

Adonis flowers	福寿草
prim rose flowers	桜草と
Bloom at each place	それぞれの軒

A yellow daffodil	黄水仙
This year again	今年また
In breezes chilly	寒き微風
In pale the light yellow	黄淡く
Sways	揺る

Chapter3 Bulbul Bird

三章　ひよ鳥

In Musashino	武蔵野
It getting dark	静かに
Calm	暮れゆくも
Yellow daffodils	黄水仙
Sway	揺る

Yellow daffodils	黄水仙
In chilly winds	寒風のなか
Turned into daffodils	ラッパ水仙と
Like trumpets	なりゆく

Japanese Peony	牡丹
The buds	苔
Come to open	開きゆく
Including	時
Time	含みをり

A mangolia flower	木蓮の奥
On the deepest bottoms	仏
Buddha	住まい
Living	居り

Red plum blossoms	紅梅は
Behind white plum ones	白梅の奥
Faintly to be seen	うっすらと

Cypress leaves   桧葉
In the sunshine leaks through trees   木洩れ日に
When white plum blossoms   白梅の
Falling down   散りてゆく

I picked up   拾いたる
Oriental elm fruit   椋の実
A bird's shadow passed away   鳥の影

Oriental elm fruit   椋の実
Stepped on and crashed   踏みしだかるゝ
On the path   小道
In sunshine deep leaking through   木洩れ日深く
trees   鳥の声
Bulbul birds twitter   冴ゆ
Clear

I picked up   拾いたる
A torreya fruit   かやの実
The one   一つ
Green and bitter   青き渋き
The scent of   古里の
My hometown   香り

Alone	一人
I am walking	ゆく果て
At the end	彼岸花
Cluster amaryllis flowers	咲き
Bloom	水
Water	流れゆく
Flows clear	

All of my life	全て
I leave	運命に
To my destiny	まかせ居る
Now for a moment	今一時の
A peace for me	安らぎ

You	君
Purchased to take home	買い来し
So big	大きなる
The half a radish	半分の大根
Now so dear	いとし

A fig tree	無花果
Goes grow up	伸びゆく
Piling up	幾度かの
So many times	思い
My wishes	重ねつつ

Piling up	幾度かの
Not a few times	思い
My wishes	重ねつつ
Now	今
Fig leaves	無花果の葉
Falling down	散りゆく

All things	すべて
I lost	失いたるもの
Overlapping	重なりて

In the relations	関係の中に
In the distance	その距離の
	なかに

You	君
Boil	菜花
Rape flowers' plants	茹でる
The scent	香り
Feel painful	いたいたしき

A radish flower	大根の花
Sways in wind	風に揺る
In weak purple	白きうす紫の
As hard as possible	ひたすらに
Tries to grow up	成りゆかんとす

Once onto the ground	一度は
Toppled down to lie	たおれ伏す
The radish flower	大根花
Cutting off	切りすて
All	来し
In my past	わが過去
My regrets in my mind	悔恨の
The slits deep	切れ込み深し
As fig leaves	無花果の葉
Where	居るべき
I should be	ところ
Before I know when	いつの間にか
I am there	居る
My place is	新しき
Where	生命
A new life	生まれいづる
To be born	方に居る
The rape flower	菜の花の
Yellow color tender	黄の優しさ
Because of you	君ゆえに

You pick	君摘む
Rape flowers	菜の花の
The one is for	一つは
Your hair ornament	髪かざり
Because of you	君故に
My loneliness sad	悲しき孤独
Because of you	君ゆえに
I get healed	癒さるゝ
Swiss chard grass	普段草
In a garden	君と僕の
For you and me	庭に
Grows	生う
Tulips	前に居た人
Former resident	植えゆきし
Planted and moved out	チューリップ
They boom out and	咲き
Now come falling	今散りゆく
In our garden	君と僕の庭
For the first one	まず小さき
A tiny rape flower	菜の花
Bloomed out	一つ咲き

I like to see	我迎う
The yellow color	菜の花の
In the rape flower	黄の
So tender	優しさよ
Cherry blossoms	桜
Start to bloom	咲きそめる
The blue sky	青空
Hazy	淡く
Cherry blossoms	桜
Swaying	揺らし
The setting sun	夕日
Goes sinking	ゆく
Cherry blossoms	桜
Overlapping each other	うち重なりて
Going hazy	霞みゆく
Cherry blossoms	桜
To the blizzard	ふぶく方に
Go	ゆく

Spring breathing	春息吹く
In Musashino	武蔵野
Oak's treetop	楢こずえ
Dark and light	濃く淡く
Into light pink	うす紅
Dyed	染むる

Magnolia kobus flowers	こぶし
Open	咲く
On a hill side	山腹の
Peaceful	穏やかに
Mountain birds	山鳥のいる

On a mountain side	山腹の
Magnolia kobus flowers	こぶし咲く
High up budding	上
Wild cherry blossoms	山桜萌ゆ

All over the mountain	全山
Budding out while	萌ゆる中
Magnolia kobus flowers	こぶし花
Come falling down	散りゆく

In the spring dawn   春暁の
Singing of a bush warbler   鶯の声
My conscience   我が良心の
Suffers to pain   やみ痛む

In the end of my loneliness   孤独のはて
Time   時
Comes clear   透きとおる

When I get aware   気がつけば
In a platform edge   ホームの果て
I am walking   歩きいる

In the dark shadow   人生の
In my life   陰影
Visible or hiding   見え隠れする
The truth is   真実

Towards   見え来る
Coming visible   方に
I go   行く

The bottom of existence   存在の底
Comes visible to me   見え来る

You	君
A thin mist	薄き霧
My ordeal	我が課題
To love	君を
You is	愛することは
To return it to God	神に返すこと
To return it to my blames	自らの
My awakening to love	罪に返すこと
Requiring no gains	無の愛に
	目覚め
	ゆくこと
You	君
A deep water pool	深き渕
My ordeal	我が課題
Chasing me	我
You come running	追い来るは
On a sidewalk	君
Cherry blossoms	桜散る
Falling on	歩道
You are here	君あり
I am here	我ある
A mystery	不思議

A Himalayan cedar   ヒマラヤ杉
Over the swaying treetop   梢揺る果て
Far beyond the bush   森林の
The blue sky and clouds   青空と
                                     雲

In Musashino   武蔵野の
Into the fresh green trees   新緑の奥
At the end a bird's old nest   古き鳥の巣
I found   一つ

Beside the window   窓辺
A Himalayan cedar   ヒマラヤ杉
Swaying in the afternoon   揺る丶午後
You graduated   君卒業す

You   君
A thin mist   薄きミスト
Wearing   かかる
A spring sprite   春の妖精
Turns into   看護婦姿と
A nurse figure   なりてゆく

In the early spring	早春の
Warm is light	暖かき光あれど
Though	冷たき風
Still cold are winds	武蔵野の高き梢
High tree tops in Musashino	思いがけず鋭き啄木鳥の声
Unexpectedly sharp	その姿探し見上げれば
Cries of a woodpecker	やはり早春の青空
Searching for him when I look up	切なくはやき雲
As usual the blue sky	流れゆく
Clouds run too fast	
To go flow	

White	白き
Flower buds	花蕾
Orange flowers	ミカン花
Fragrant	香る

In Musashino	武蔵野の
Dandelions	タンポポ
Picking you	摘む君
In the white gown	白衣
Red cross	赤十字の

You	君
An orange flower	ミカン花
A faint scent	ほのか香る
Your white gown	白衣
Red cross	赤十字
Under the blue sky	青空に
Swaying	揺る
Akebia flowers	木通花
My regrets	我が悔恨の
Spreading in my heart	胸に滲み
Painful	痛む
The blue sky in a distant	遠き青空
One line of	飛行機雲の
A vapor trail	一すじ
Starling birds	椋鳥も
Turtledoves hop	雉鳩もいて
In Musashino	武蔵野
In the early summer	初夏の
Grass fields	草原

Looking back   来た道

At the path I came walking   振り返り

To see the early summer   見れば

In Musashino   武蔵野の

The sun shines leaking through   初夏

trees   木洩れ日

Chapter4 Moment

四章　一瞬

This morning	今朝は
Sparrows chirp	雀鳴いて
My usual mind	平常心
Setting me	我を
Into right	正しゆく

I again	また
Stretch up	背筋
My backbones	伸ばしいる
To me	我に
Fresh green	新緑
May winds	五月風

Leaves of cherry blossoms	葉桜の
The veins	葉脈
So Robust	たくましき

My destiny	運命と
The Inevitability	必然の
In the live oak's lodge	樫の宿
Now	今
The time comes on	時現れて
Pomegranate flowers	ざくろ花
Bloom out	咲く

This one moment   この　時も

Eternity   永遠

Leaves of cherry blossoms   葉桜

In the sun leaking though trees   木もれ日の

The path   道

In the live oak's lodge   樫の宿

I am living here   我ここに生き

Now by my side   見取るは

You   君

Twenty-two years old   二十二

Beside the window   窓辺さらに

So lovable   いとけなき

One   ざくろ実

Pomegranate fruit   一つ

You   君

Came back   抱き

Holding   帰り来し

Yellow   黄の

Miniature roses   ミニバラの

Flowers   花は

In two centimeters   二センチ程の

May winds	五月風
Blow	吹いて
I am	我
Getting afresh	改まりゆく
You	汝
A yellow	黄の
Miniature rose	ミニバラ
My regrets	わが悔恨の
Pains	胸の
In my mind	痛み
Not to be made up	埋めやらず
Outside	外
It is calm	静まりて
A bird twitters	鳥鳴く
Consoling me	我
To some extent	慰める
Good	程よき
A throng of people	雑踏

This evening	今宵
My consolation is	慰めは
Thou	汝
A yellow	黄の
Miniature rose	ミニバラ
Alone	唯一つ
Playing	モーツアルトの音
The sound of Mozart	奏でいる

In a cafe	カフェ
When a person leaves	人たつとき
Do I also to	我もたつ
Leave?	ときか

In a station	駅
Steps for	雑踏の階段
So many people	灰色の影
In the swaying gray shadows	揺れるなか
Someone sighs	誰か溜息

One by one	人
Different	それぞれに
From	我と
Me	異なる
Persons	人々
Console me	我を慰める

Pumpkin flowers	カボチャ花
The yellow color	黄の
Peaceful to me	安らぎてある
In the morning	午前
I parted from you	君と別れゆく

Pumpkin's	カボチャ
The first flower	初花の
Yellow	黄の
Before noon	昼またず
Withered	しほみゆく

With	サフランと
A saffron flower	過ごす
I spend	秋の午後
In the afternoon	サフランの
In autumn	影
The shadow	

Dark shadow	暗き闇
Impossible	超えることの
To cross over	出来ぬ水
The water	川
The river	流れをり
Flows	

A morning glory	朝顔
Opens out	一つ咲き
Vines	蔓
Parted	別れをり

Loving together	愛し合う
In the end	はて
I hear bulbuls	ひよ鳥の声
In the distance	遠く
Twitter	鳴く

A river	川すじ
Parted	二手に
Into two	別れ
Then again	また合いて
Unified to run	ゆく

To part	別るゝには
Too much	あまりに
Big a	大き
Relation	関わり

My silent　　　　　　無言の

Meal　　　　　　　　食事

A bulbul bird　　　　ひよ鳥

A cry in a distant　　遠く鳴く

A distance　　　　　君との

From you　　　　　距離

Loneliness　　　　　淋しさと

And freedom　　　　自由

Wanting to stand up　席たたんと

From my seat　　　　思えど

At the time　　　　　今

My melody　　　　　我が

I hear　　　　　　　メロディ

　　　　　　　　　　聞こえ来る

Now　　　　　　　　今

I hear　　　　　　　鳴るは

Lonesome　　　　　わびしき

Sounds of an oboe　オーボエ

In Musashino | 武蔵野の
A path of fall leaves | 落葉道
Like my life | わが人生のごと
It goes forward | 行きつ
It turns back | 戻りつ

In Musashino | 武蔵野の
Falling leaves | 落葉
Resemble me | 我に似たる
One leaf | 一つ
I picked up | 拾いにけり

A box-leaf holly tree | もちの木
Still green | まだ青き
The berries | 実の
In some time | いづれ
Turning into red | 赤くなりゆく
Should be | はずの

Now | 今
A bulbul bird | ひよ鳥
Flies up | 飛びたつ
A cry for a moment | 一瞬の声

In chilly winds	寒風のなか
I picked up	拾いし
One fallen leaf	落葉一つ
Into my breast pocket	胸ポケットに
Light of Christmas	クリスマスの灯
On and off	明滅す
In my life	わが人生の
What I gained	得しもの
What I lost	失いしものと
Christmas	クリスマス
Passed	過ぎて
Yet still	なお
Light on and off	明滅する灯
With no changes	かわりなく
Living	生きている
I am	我

This evening   今宵

For my consolation   慰めは

One   椰子の実

Coconut fruit   一つ

In Musashino   武蔵野に

Year's eve coming closer   師走寄る

In the light   灯のもと

In a throng of people   雑踏の中

Life's   人生の

Sweet liquor and   甘酒と

Bitter liquor   渋酒と

Mixing I drink   混じり飲む

The window pane   窓

Clouded and wet   曇りぬれる

High up a faint   上わずか

Blue sky in winter   冬の青空

Birds fly across   鳥渡りゆく

Today   今日

Rain falls   降る雨

On live oak leaves   樫の葉の

Icy raindrops   冷たき雫

Live oak leaves	樫の葉
Live oak leaves' raindrops	樫の葉の雫
Sway	揺る
The one drop	一雫
Eternity	一瞬の
In an instant	永遠
Live oak leaves'	樫の葉の
Water drops stop	雫やみ
A clarified	清められたる
Calm	静けさ
Life is	人生の
A sorrowful	悲しき
Revolving lantern	走馬灯
Now lights on my blames	今ともるは
On my lack of power	罪と無力と
At a crossroad of life	人生の岐路
What I get	得るものと
What I lose	失うものと
In the valley	谷間
Go flowing	流れゆく

Under an iron bridge	鉄橋の
On the river shore	河原
Wild roses	野いばら
Bloom out	咲く

In my life	人生
I step out of	良心を
Conscience	踏み外しゆく
In the end	はて

My shoelaces	靴ヒモ
Half the pair	片方
Undone	ほどけいたる

After you left	君去りてのち
The window	窓
All the time cloudy	曇りをり

A gardenia	くちなし
Flower fragrant	花香る
When I move	我一人
Alone by myself	動くたび

On the relationship	関わりと
On the distance	距離と
Clouds I wipe	曇り拭く
Outside the window	窓外
Pomegranates	ざくろ
Are all wet	濡れいる
In my loneliness	わが孤独
Tall is a tree of	高き
Ever green magnolia	泰山木
The fragrance	芳香は
Goes into a blue sky	青空の中
Pomegranate flowers	ざくろ花
Looking up	上向きて
Bloom out	咲くも
Looking down	下向きて
Bloom out	咲くも
Equals	等しき
In the sun leaks through trees	木洩れ日の中

Today	今日
In a rainy season	梅雨
Raindrops	雨雫
From pomegranate flowers	ざくろ花より
Dropping down	落つ
No longer	これ以上
Any destinations for me	行き着く所なき
My thinking	わが思い
Now	今に
Comes up to be most	極まる
On a smallest	小さき
Fern	シダの
Leaf	一葉にも
Mountain winds	山風の
Blow swaying	吹き揺る、
In Musashino	武蔵野の
Fallen leaves	落ち葉
Scattered	散り
And whirling up	舞いあがる
A fallen leaf of	君と僕の
You and me	落ち葉
We pick up again	また拾う

Balsam flowers   鳳仙花

Stalks and roots red   茎根赤く

The shadow of leaves   葉影

To be transparent   透けゆく

Chapter5 Pomegranate Flowers

五章　ざくろ花

A storm gone	嵐去りて
Welling up	清水
Clear water	湧き出づる
The sound	音

In a shrine	神社木陰より
In the shadow of trees	汲み来たる
I draw clear water up	清水にて
So I am spending	今日夏の
Today hot in the summer	午後
In the afternoon	過ごさんとぞ
Cool with the water	思う

Alone	一人
I go to draw	清水
Clear water	汲みにゆく

Cool	冷たき
Fresh water	真水
I fill it in my mouth	口に含み
To gulp down	飲み下す

The stream to flow	流れ来る
With water sounds	水音
Jumpseed flowers	水引草
Open	咲き

In Musashino	武蔵野の
In the shadow of trees	木陰
My shadows is	わが影
Close to the tree's	木によりそいて
Shadow	あり

I wonder why	何故か
Dry twig	枯れ枝と
Green acorn	青どんぐりと
Drop together?	共に落つ

From the seaside	海より
I came back	戻りたる
On the morning	あした
In Musashino	武蔵野に
Tit birds	四十雀
Twittering	鳴く

In the end	運命の
Of the fate	果て
Purple color	朝顔の
Of morning glories	紫
Are calm	静まりて
	あり

On the morning	旅より
When came back	戻りたる
From travel	あした
Morning glory	朝顔の
The purple color	紫
Transparent	透き通る

You are here	君居る
The purple color	朝顔の
Of morning glory	紫

Turning	角
At the corner	まがれば
White powder flowers	白粉花
In our live oak's lodge	樫の宿

Smell of grass	草いきれ
From somewhere	どこからか
A hazy moon there	おぼろ月
In Musashino	武蔵野の
Over our live oak's lodge	樫の宿

Thinking of something	もの思いつ
You	君
Brought back	持ち帰り来しは
White powder flowers	白粉花
Faint	かすか
Light pink	薄紅の

Balsam flowers	鳳仙花
Single-petaled	一重
I bought	求むれど
This year	今年
Double-petaled flowers	八重咲く
Bloom out	

This year	今年
Balsam flowers	鳳仙花
Double-petaled	八重
Just fit	わが心
To my mind	埋むるに
To be buried	合う

Balsam flowers	鳳仙花
Growing to bloom	咲きのぼり
This year	今年
The summer	夏
Goes passing	過ぎゆく
Balsam flowers	鳳仙花
Turn transparent	透けゆく
Beyond	時の
Time	彼方
Watermelon vine	西瓜蔓
Plucking a bud	芽摘めば
The female flower	小さき実の
With a berry	雌花
Bearing	あるものを
At a full moon night	満月の夜
My conscience	良心の
Again	さらに
Feeling sick	やみゆく

The full moon	満月
Passed over	過ぎゆきて
Now into a half moon	半月の
The moon at midnight	夜半の月

In the summer	夏
Why?	何故か
Colored leaves	落ち葉
Constantly	絶え間なく
Falling down	落つ下
Under them	我
I walked on	行けり

More than usual	いつもより
So many	多く
Colored leaves falling	落ち葉散る
That day in the early autumn	かの初秋の日
Green acorns	青どんぐりも
Dropped down	散りをりし

The river	川
In the shallow	瀬
Waves in blue and white	青く白く
Swirling	逆まき
No more returning	帰らざる
My past time	わが過去
Runs there	流れゆく

Where	青き水
Blue water	白く
Into white	泡だち
Bubbling up	ゆくところ

The river	川
Leaving shallows behind	瀬残し
Goes flow	流れゆく

A white dot	白き点
Moving or	動いているのか
Not moving?	いないのか
I watch it the more	見つむれば
The more it be unclear	見つむる程

Whcrc	川面
Water surface	さざ波たつ
Ripples up	ところ

Over my grave	我が墓の上に
Pine winds rustle	松風鳴り
Bunting birds	頬白さえずり
Twitter	下草に
In the glass benieth	桔梗花
Bell flowers	揺る
Sway	

May be one teardrop	一露の涙あらん
For my vain life	はかなき生

The river	川
The shallows	瀬
Where	水くだけたる
Water is broken	ところ

My past	過去すでに
Is gone now	あらず
Though the present is there	今あるも
In an instant	瞬時
It becomes the past	過去となる
Where is my life?	わが生いづこ
It ended already?	すでに
	終わりたるか
In the empty	はかなき
Time	時間の中に
Into nothingness	無の中へと
Not can be permitted but	許され得ない
Shall I destroy myself?	自己破滅をなすか
Or from the depths in my despair	その絶望の渕より
Again return to what I am	再び自己本来に立ち返り
To live winning eternal life?	永遠なるものとしての生を
	獲得し生きるか
Why	何故に
Does God	神
Your divinity	神性を
Reveal?	現わす
Water shines	水光り
Rippling	さざめく
The angle	角度

Something eternal　　　　　永遠なるものに
To be touched　　　　　　触れゆく

The angle of life　　　　　生きる角度
Always and usually　　　　ひたすらに
Exists　　　　　　　　　　いる

Nature's　　　　　　　　　自然の
Beauty and　　　　　　　　美と
Order is　　　　　　　　　秩序
In bush clovers　　　　　　萩にも
In butterflies　　　　　　　蝶にも

In nature's　　　　　　　　自然の
Order　　　　　　　　　　秩序
Flying　　　　　　　　　　飛びゆく
A flock of　　　　　　　　群れ
Plovers　　　　　　　　　千鳥

A first dragonfly　　　　　初トンボ
Comes　　　　　　　　　　来て
Reperches　　　　　　　　止まり直す

On my small bamboo	わが篠竹に
A dragonfly	トンボ
Resting	止まりいる
I feel happy	幸せ

Pomegranete fruits	ざくろ実
In the calmness	静かなる
The one swaying	一つ揺れ
Now I am	我今
In the live oak's lodge	樫の宿に
Living on	住まいをり

Gourd bottle flower	夕顔
The one	一輪
Why?	何故か
Towards the late autumn	晩秋に
Bloom out	向けて
	咲く

In the late autumn	晩秋に
A tiny	小さき
Fig fruit	無花果の
	実

A vapor's trail of airplane	飛行機雲
Splitting into	一すじ
The autumn sky	秋空に
To vanish away	切れ込み
	消えゆく
External appearance	外面は
God gave	神が与えしもの
Internal mind	内面は
The more	さらに
Can link	神に
With God	つながりゆくもの
When I ask	問えば
You ask back	問い返し来る
With your eyes	君が視線
When you come	君来れば
Time shows up	時現れる
With you	君と
My talking	語りをる
Time accumulated	時重なりて
Into infinity	無限となる

Chapter6　Balsam Flowers

六章　鳳仙花

Fallen leaves	落ち葉
Piled now	多くなりゆく
I walk on	我歩く
Just like it a path	道らしく

Fallen leaves	落ち葉
I am walking on	わが
My landmarks	歩きゆき
	道しるべ

Yesterday with you	昨日
I sowed seeds	君と
Today	種まきし
Quietly	今日
Rain falls	静かなる
In Musashino	武蔵野の雨

Quiet rain falls	しめやかに
In Musashino	武蔵野の
On the soil	雨
In Musashino	武蔵野の土

In my hometown	古里の
Pine trees resound	松風鳴る
Seeds scattered	木の実
	散りをり

82

You starling	椋鳥
From where	いづこより
Came pecking them?	啄み来たる

Japanese laurel fruit	青木の実
Small and	幼く
Tiny	小さきに
Leaves are	落葉
Falling on it	散りかかる

A light aircraft	軽飛行機
For a moment	一瞬
The shadow passing over	影よぎり
Then leaving	去りゆく
The sounds	音

Crossing	信号
At the signal	渡る
You	君
For a moment	一瞬の
Receiving	我が視線
My sight	受け止めて
	ゆく

On sidewalks	歩道の
Cosmos flowers	コスモス
Feeling like sensing a walker	人の気配
Sway	揺る
The acordion	シャンソンの
Playing chanson	アコーディオン
Swaying	コスモス花
Cosmos flowers	揺らし
	ゆく
In the autumn wind	秋風
A bronze	ブロンズの
Girl	少女
An empty can	空きカン
Comes rolling	わが前に
Just before me	ころがり
To be	来て
Settled	定まりぬ
Before I get aware	何時しか
A seat	賑わいの
Beside me	わがかたわらの
Turned bustling	席

Waves calm	波静かなる
On the beach	水際
Tiny shellfish	小さき貝
Faint	かそけき
Fish shadows	魚影

Waves approaching	波寄する
On the beach	水際
Plover birds	千鳥
Step marks	あしあと
Running	走る

Light	光
Comes on	及び来る
At my foot	足元に
Waves	波くだけ
Broken	ゆく

A sea bird	海鳥の
Hovers in air	静止したる
In the pose	ままに
He flying	飛び居たる

Tides full	潮満ち
Uprising	上げくれば
I wonder	帰る道
My return way	いづれかと
Which?	思う

Seagulls fly	カモメ飛び
The tides sounds	水音の
Even now I hear	今もする

Time	君と僕の
For you and me	時
Eternal	永遠なり

Before me	わが前
Growing through	すり抜けて
Loofha vines	ヘチマ
Flowers open	咲く

Moon flowers vines	夕顔
From the next garden	隣より
Come stretching over	伸び来たり
Opening	咲く

At next house	隣
In the window	窓辺
Light off	灯消えて
Sounds of	時
Ticking time	刻む音
Sounds of	虫
Chirping insects	鳴く音
Still in my solitude	わが淋しさのままに
Autumn winds blow	秋の風
Where birds twitter	鳥の声
A location	君と僕の
For you and me	位置
Every time	その都度
New	新しき
Time	時
Having	積み重なりて
Piled up	来る

Time shall	時
Never end	終わることなく
Tit birds shall	四十雀
Come up again	またくる
Every time	その都度
Time shows up	時現れて
To be endless	無限となる
Constantly	絶えず
In eternity	永遠の中に
Always and anytime	ひたすらに
To live	居る
Fragrant olive trees	木犀の香
Tiny	小さき
Flowers	花々の
In infinity	永遠
Malabar nightshade	蔓むらさきの
Purple	つる
The vine	紫の

Scensing	晩柑の
Bankan orange	香りかげば
Orange flower	ミカン花
Fragrant	香る

Malabar nightshade vines	つる紫の
The flower buds	花荅
Tiny	小さき
Light purple	薄むらさきの

Malabar nightshade vines	つる紫
Grew stretching	伸び上がりたる
In the last	先の
Late autumn	晩秋

One stretch of	一筋の篠竹
Small bamboo	一蔓の
One vine of	朝顔
Morning glory	

A vine of morning glory	朝顔のつる
From the edge of the small bamboo	篠竹のはて
Stretching up into air	伸び上がる

A vine of morning glory   思案する
Wondering how?   朝顔のつる
On the top   先

Fresh   新しき
Water   水
You   ポットに
Pouring   注しゆく
Into a jar   君

For what a purpose   何の為の
My life is?   生

To live through   矛盾を
Contradictions   生きる

Though in sadness   悲しくも
I make steps forward   進む

For the purpose   その為の
Unhappiness   不幸

My road distant	遠き道
With the past and	過去と
Premonitions for future	予感と
The more sad	悲しければ
The more clear	悲しい程
Coming into my view	見え来る
Something floating up	浮かび来るもの
I proceed into the direction	見え来る方に
Coming into my view	行く
Depths of existence	存在の底
Come into my view	見え来る
In God's	神の意図
Iintentions	ありて
I again start	また求め
Questing for	ゆく

I am	我
Some existence	湧き出づる
Welling out	もの
Awaken from	眠りより
Sleeping	覚むれば
I find	我
Again	また
Myself alive	生きてをり
When I awake	覚むれば
Again	また
I try to live on	生きゆく
When I have no purpose	人生
In my life	無目的となりぬ
In the blue sky	青空
A moon floats up	月浮かぶ
The sky is blue	青空
The blue color	青
Pointing at	無限の彼方
Infinity in a far distant	指す

Chapter7 Fig Tree

七章　無花果

Sea of Izu	伊豆の海
So warm	暖かき
Into mountains	山間に
Entering to see	入りて見ゆ

Pink shells and	桜貝に
Plover birds	千鳥
The step marks	足あと

So great	大いなる
A joy of the sea!	海の歓喜
Light dazzling	光眩しき海
With no borders	区別なく
With no ends	果てしなく
Far beyond time	時の彼方

Picking summer oranges	夏みかんもぐ
In a village of Izu	伊豆の里
Less than two	二つよりは
We should pick	取り過ぎと
You say	君

Blue tides	青き潮
Overflowing	満ちあふる
Quiet	静かなる
Over	富士壺の
Barnacles	上

Sea birds	海鳥
Come closer	寄り来たりて
And leave off	去る

At starboad	右舷
Light so bright	光眩しき
In the sea	海

Off the shore	沖合に
Two boats	舟二艘
Faintly	かすか
Swaying	揺れいる
The setting sun	夕陽
Dazzling	眩しき
Far beyond time	時の彼方

At the house I left	我去りし家
Confederate roses	芙蓉
Blooming	咲きをり
My returning back	元に
Impossible	戻ることは
I think	出来ないと思う
Clusters amaryllis flowers	彼岸花
Bloom and fall	咲き散り
Green sprouts	青き芽
Come up	出づ
My planting bulbs	球根植える我
The house I left	去りし家
Gone far from me now	遠くなりにけり
All in the late autumn	晩秋すべて
Withering sounds	枯れゆくものゝ音
A shadow of bird	鳥影
In a moment	一瞬
Falls down	落つ

Even say a storm   嵐と言うも
Belongs to this world   この世のもの

Falling to spread   散り敷く
Leaves into patterns   落ち葉模様
Life is   人生
A beauty of disturbance   波乱の美
It reflects to my eyes   目に映り
Piecing through my mind   心に染みる

One streak of   けむり
Smoke   一すじに
Going up   立ちのぼり
To the high   ゆく

You left   君去りて
Red cross   赤十字
Leaves scattered   晩秋の落葉
In the late autumn   散りけり

Leaves   落ち葉
Fallen in a carpet   散り敷きて
Saffron flowers   サフラン
Come out   咲く

Saffron flowers	サフランの
Red pistils	しべ赤き
On the top	先
Yellow	黄の
Pollen	花粉

Only the one	一すじ
Shines	光る
In the autumn	秋
A spider's thread	蜘蛛の糸

In vain	空しき
I drink water	水飲む
The bottom of my glass	グラスの底
Swaying	揺る

Tramps	浮浪者の
Enjoy gathering	団らん
In the dusk of autumn	秋の黄昏

Human weakness	人間の弱さ
Clearing out	透き通る
A vagabond	浮浪者の
Plays the guitar	ギター弾き

The sea of Boso	房総の海
Quiet	穏やかに
In mountains	山
Cicadas singing loud	蟬しぐれ
Falling	ゆく

Your	君が
Hat	帽子
On my knee	わが膝の上
A brown ribbon	茶のリボン
So long	長くして

Near the sea station	海駅近く
Yellow canna flowers	黄のカンナ
Bloom in a cluster	群れ咲きて

Your	君
Hat	帽子
A brown ribbon	茶のリボン
Writing poems	もの書く
You a girl	少女

For a view of the blue sea	青き海へ
On a sea wall	防波堤
To the edge	先端

Traveling bags	旅のカバン
Two	二つ
Stand side by side	並びいて

First singing of	はじめての
A meimuna opelifara cicada	つくつく法師
In a traveling inn	旅の宿

You	君
Have white skin	白き肌
With hands peeling pears	梨むく手

In a travel inn	旅の宿
Oreander flowers	夾竹桃の
Bloom	咲く

Nojimazaki cape	野島崎
The sea is	海
A sign of God	神の印
Light from the lighthouse	灯台の灯
A Christ's sign of love	十字架のキリストの
On the Cross	愛の印

At the inn of Onjuku 御宿の宿
While our sleeping breaths 寝息
Melt 溶け入る間
Sea birds shriek 海鳥の鳴く

The sea resounding 海鳴しつゝ
One night 一晩の
"On the Desert of the Moon*" 月の砂漠

* A popular song for children, made in Japan.
A prince and a princess on camels go riding on the desert.
In the beach of Onjuku, the statues stand.

On returning 朝市より
From a morning market 戻る
To our traveling inn 旅の宿
Kite birds cry トンビ鳴く

Closed in the sea lodge 雷雨に
Attacked by the thundering storm 降り込められて
We are talking together 海の家
Over the sweets of フルーツみつ豆と
Fruit honey beans コーヒーと
And cups of coffee 語り合う

Hot water welling sounds	湯湧く音
Winds' sounds	風の音
On the bottom of hot water	湯の底も
A lonely	孤独なる
Shadow	影
Diving into	湯の底に
The bottom of hot water	潜るも
Only one shadow of mine	我が影一つ
Getting lost	迷いつつ
To return	たちかえり
Lost again	また迷い
To return	立ちかえる
In my regrets	悔恨の
A revolving lantern	走馬灯の
Beside the window	窓辺
The past	過去
Not becoming	過去と
Into the past	なりゆかず
I stand still	我佇む

Asakawa river	浅川の
The water shore	水際
Now gone	遠く
To a far distant	絶えゆく
In my sorrow	悲し
Long time ago	かの昔
With my wife	妻と
I enjoyed much	遊びし
There	

White	フリージャの
Freesia flowers	白
My wife when she was with me	別れし
Liked so much	妻の
	好みし

My Korea is	わが朝鮮
Inside me	我が内なる
Being gone to disappear	自然のままに
As if it be natural	絶えゆく

On a mountain side	山腹に
Blooming	咲き
Falling down but	散り
Starting to sprout out again	萌えゆく
The magnolia kobus blossoms	こぶし花

A lonely　　　　　　　　　淋しさの

Crescent moon　　　　　　三日月

With a star　　　　　　　　星と

Supporting each other　　　支え合う

Chapter8 Gojiberry

八章　枸杞の実

Citrus fruit　　　　　　　柚子
The last　　　　　　　　　今年
Time　　　　　　　　　　 最後の
In this year　　　　　　　時
Fragrant　　　　　　　　 香る

In the year's eves　　　　年の瀬に
Magnolia kobus　　　　　こぶし
Flower buds　　　　　　　花苔

Evergreen magnolia tree　泰山木の
The fragrance　　　　　　芳香は
Rising up over roof tiles　屋根瓦越え
Into the blue sky　　　　　青空の中

In an instant　　　　　　一瞬
A bird shadow passed away　鳥影よぎる
I looked up to see　　　　 朝の窓
The morning window　　 見上げれば
Wet all over with dewdrops　曇り濡れる
Running down in their ways　露の道
　　　　　　　　　　　　　幾すじ

Today rain falls
Cold raindrops down
from the live oak leaves
Just like in my regrets

今日降る雨
樫の葉の
わが悔恨の
冷たき雫

Like my destiny
Raindrops
From the oak leaves
Fall down

運命の
雨雫
樫の葉より
落つ

Live oak leaves
Raindrops on them
Sway

樫の葉
樫の葉の雫
揺る

From on the oak leaves
Falling raindrops stopped
Purified
Quietness

樫の葉の
雫やみ
清められたる
静けさ

At a life's crossroad
What I gained
What I lost
Go flowing
In the valley

人生の岐路
得るものと
失うものと
谷間
流れゆく

Green signal	青信号
The light on and off	点滅し
Again turns red	また赤

In a cafe	雑踏の
Crowded	カフェ
"I am	私が
To blame	悪いの
Sorry"	ゴメンネ
I happened to hear	ふと聞こゆ
The speech still	その言葉
Remaining in me	我に残りぬ

Someone	誰か
Left to go	忘れゆきし
A telephone card	テレホンカード
Phalaenopsis orchids	絵柄は
Illustrated	コチョウラン

A wrecker	レッカー
Towing	移動されゆく
A car	車
Fate powerless	運命の無力
My sorrow	悲しさよ

In destiny
Rain in the rainy season
Pomegranate flowers
Receiving

わが運命の
つゆの雨
ざくろ花
受く

The wind blows
Also
Rain falls

風吹いて
やはり
雨降る

Cluster amaryllis flowers
In bloom
Coming to flow
Water sounds

彼岸花
咲き
流れ来る
水音

Jumpseed flowers
Blooming

水引草
咲く

Stream of water
The flowing sounds
Time going to leave
The sounds

水
流れゆく音
時去りゆく
音

Only   ただ
In an instant   一瞬の
Now this moment 今

Full star flowers   満天星の
Faintly   ほのか
Fragrant   花香る
From you   君

With your hands   君が手
You chop parsley   指幼きままに
Your fingers young パセリ
As they are   刻む

Fragant olive blossoms 金木犀
Fragrant   香る
In eternity   永遠

The moment   永遠に
I touch   触れる
Eternity   瞬間

Eternal   永遠の
This moment   今

My reaching point	到達点
This moment	今
Now	すでに
Eternal	永遠
My sight	わが視界
Grows up	生い育ち
Sways	揺るゝ
All	全て
God's holy spirit	神の聖霊
The Iruma River	入間川
My past	わびしき
Solitary	わが過去
Now	今
With no water	水なき
It flows	流れをり
Last night	昨夜
In my sad time	悲しき時間
A winter star	冬の星
Twinkling	またゝきて
Passed away	過ぎにけり

Lights on Christmas	クリスマスの灯
As they were	そのままに
On and off	明滅する
Reflecting on a window	ウィンドー
Just like me	わがごとき
In a sorrow	淋しさの

Christmas	クリスマスの
Lights	灯
With red leaves	わずか
Barely	残りたる
Left	紅葉と

Absent lamp	留守ランプ
Still as it is	そのままに
Calm and	静まりて
Quiet	あり

Someone comes back	人帰り来る
The stepping sounds	音
At the next door	隣の

A fluorescent light	蛍光灯
Slightly	かすか
Sways	揺れいる
Alone I am	一人

From a small space through	狭き
the door	ドアの隙間より
I see outside is there another light	外にまた灯ありて

In Musashino	武蔵野の
On a narrow path	小道
I walk	我歩む
I walked	歩みし道

Gojiberry	枸杞の実
Barely	わずか
Left	残りし

Tumbled down	たおれ
On the ground	伏す
A radish flower	大根花
From there	そこより
Stands up	立つ

Thinking	人生の
On life	思索
Refreshed	新た
On the way of cherry trees in leaf	葉桜の道

In Musashino	武蔵野の
A narrow way in my memory	思い出の細き小道
Walking up the little hill	登り来て
When looking back	振り返り見れば
My empty past	わが空しき過去
The setting sun	落日
Like blood melting into clouds	血のごとく雲にとけ
Evening smokes are trailing	夕の煙たなびきてをり

A distant thunder	遠雷や
Around the place where you are	君いるあたり
Trailing	辿りゆく

A big star and	大き星
Another one	一つ
Twinkling bright	また一つ
You are	輝きて
Protected	君
Surely	守られてをり

Your forehead   君が額
Young   幼き
Faintly white   仄白き
Wearing a nurse cap   ナースキャップ
Red cross   赤十字の

Chapter9　Remaining Shadow

九章　残影

After you left me	君
I have	去りてのち
Empty awakening	ポッカリと
	目覚む
Saffron flowers fell down	サフラン散り
Saffron	サフラン
Growing up	伸びゆく
Crocus	クロッカス
Sprouting	芽
Out	出づる
After	サフランの
Saffron	のち
Trains	電車
Going down	下りゆく
Ears of pampas grass	すすき穂
Swaying	揺る
This morning	今朝は
Bulbul birds	ひよ鳥
Flying to cry	飛びつ鳴くなる
Cries go jumping	鳴き声飛び飛びに
Scattered	散りゆきて

When talking
With you
The setting sun
Fully sinking down

君と
語りし
西日
一杯に
傾きて

The setting sun
Sinking
Bush warblers
Sing

西日
傾き
藪鶯の
鳴く

One dewdrop
Each time
Momentary
Eternity

一雫
その都度の
一瞬の
永遠

One drop
Bitter
Sour
Yet having slightly
Sweetness

一雫
苦き
渋き
かすかなる
甘味

Drops
Receiving
I live

雫
受け止めて
生く

Blue sky	青空
High up	高く
Bunting birds twitter	頬白さえずる
Dogwood	花水木
The fruit	実
Red	赤く

Cherry blossoms bloom	桜咲く
On a platform	ホーム
To the end	果てまで
I go walk	歩きゆく

Today	今日
Windy and rainy	風雨
Over the way	葉桜の
Cherry trees in leaf	道

A way of cherry trees in a leaf	葉桜の道
Winds blowing	風吹いて
Rain falling	雨降る

A platform	桜咲く
Cherry blossoms bloom	ホーム
Trains	電車
Left down	下りにけり

The window in winter	冬の窓
A lake in my hometown	古里の湖
Between clouds	雲の間に
Hazily	あわく
Floating to flow	ゆく

When flower bulbs	球根の
Sprout out	芽
Shrikes	出づるに
Shriek	百舌鳥
	鳴く

For a moment	一瞬
A shadow passed	影よぎり
Sounds of	軽飛行機の
A light aircraft	音
Gone out of my hearing	消え去りて
My past	過去
Into the past	過去となり
Goes	ゆく

From the sky	曇りたる
Cloudy and in a distant	遠き空より
Snow	雪
Whirling down	舞い降りて
To mantle me	我包む

Powder snow	粉雪と
Large flakes of snow	ボタン雪と
Both together	共に
Fall down	降る
Snow flakes	雪の粒
Slightly	かすか
Drifting	舞う
In the sky clear	雪晴れの
After the snow	空
From oaks leaves	樫の葉より
Falling snowdrops	落つ雪雫
My fate	わが運命の
Freezing	冷たき
Transparent	透明
Minute	細かき
Particles	粒子
Dancing in the air	宙に舞う
In my closing eyes	目つむれど
More ones	さらに
Whirl	舞う

| Snow falling down thick | 雪降り頻る |
| Window full of dewdrops | 露の窓 |

On me in a fate	運命の我
Snow falling down thick	雪降り頻り
In a heap	降り積もる

Antennas	アンテナ
Together with snow	雪と
Slanting to topple down	落ちかかる

Snowdrops	雪雫
In the transparency	透明の
Falling down	落つ
The rhythm	リズム

In a thaw	雪溶け
Water drops	雫
Falling down	落つ
At the speed	速さ

Snow	雪
Now calm	静まりて
A bird shadow	鳥影
Flies	低く
Low	飛ぶ

Looking up	見上げれば
Even at night	夜も
Clouds	雲
In series	連なりて
Flowing	ゆく

Our fingers crossing	指切り
For a promise and	交わし
We sleep	眠る
In the night	夜
Snow	雪降り
Falling down	積む
Thick	

Chapter10 Water Drops

十章 雫

That	かの
Treetop	梢
The sky	空
Even now they are there	今もあり
In Musashino	武蔵野の
I am trailing	小道
I was trailing	我辿る
The narrow path	辿りし道

On a small shrine	祠木の
Ginkgo leaves	銀杏
Falling down	散るなり
In Musashino	武蔵野の
My walk	道

In Musashino	武蔵野の
Walking ways nostalgic	懐かしき道
When I walk along	辿りゆけば
Akebia	木通
The five-leaves in clusters	五つ葉の
Not all fallen down yet	散りやらず
A few of	枸杞の実
Gojiberry	わずか
Left	残りし

In Musashino	武蔵野の
Treetops	梢
Of zelkova trees	高槻の
Looking up	見上げれば
The winter sky	冬の空
Hazy	淡き
A half moon	半月
In white	白き
Up there	掛かりをり

In my hometown	わが古里
Raspberries	木いちごの
Still green	まだ青き
Yellow	黄色き
Berries	実の
The twigs soft	枝しなやかに
Clear water wells up	清水湧く
The shadow of leaves	仄暗き
Dim	葉陰
Even now	今も
Quietly	静かに
Water springs up	水湧き出づる

Unexpected	思わず
Cries of woodpecker	啄木鳥の声
I stop	足止め
To look up	見上げれば
Treetops high in the blue sky	梢高き青空
Clouds in the early spring	早春の雲
Fast	はや
Flow to go	流れゆく

Amaryllis flowers	暖かき
Together	光と共に
With warm light	アマリリス

Suddenly	急に
Clear up	晴れる
The winter sky	冬の空
My premonition	春
Of the spring	予感

I see from a train window	車窓
Light in a distant	遠き灯
Goes changing	移りゆく

Once	昔
The river	妻と見し
I saw with my wife	川
Suddenly	ふと
Floating up	浮かび
To flow	流れゆく

In the evening	ゆうべ
At my regretful time	苦しき時
A river of	戻ることの
No return	出来ぬ
Flows	川
	流れをり

To the past time	元には
Impossible to come back	戻れぬもの
To make detours	迂回するもの
To cross	交叉するもの
To recur	回帰するもの
To be new	新たなるもの
To manage to plan	計らうもの
In the sorrowful shadow of	罪の
Sins and blames	悲しみの
Destiny we call it	影あるもの
	運命と言うもの

What	我
I saw	見しもの
What	見えし
Is seen	もの

Things into my sight	見え来るもの
I see	見る

Where	我が
I am living	命あるところ
Light shall	光とどき
Reach	来る

On my life	命あり
Light shall	光
Come	来る

Something into my view	見え来るもの
Seeing	見る
Leaving	去りゆく
I am	我

To live	生きること
To see	見ること
To leave	去りゆくこと
In setting sun	西日受く
Daffodils	水仙
In the center	花芯
Yellow	黄
Warm	暖かく
In quietness	静まりて
Slanting	斜向きに
A daffodil	咲く
In bloom	水仙
A daffodil	花
The flower	かすか
Faint	
A daffodil flower	水仙
Before others	一輪
Goes	さきに
Passing away	絶え
	ゆかんとす

A daffodil flower	水仙
Dimly	花
Passing away	かすか
The flower center	絶えゆく
Yellow	花芯
Barely	黄
Left	僅か
	残りつ

Crowd of people	雑踏
Any body	誰も
Comforts me	我に慰めの

For a moment	一時の
Bustle	盛り上がり
Soon leaving off	去る

On my return way	帰る道
Still in my mind	心に残り
Blooms	咲く
A gardenia flower	くちなし
The many-folded petals	八重花

On the bank in a station 　　駅の上手
Mowing grass 　　草刈る
The scent 　　香
Entering the train 　　車内にも

Chinquapin flowers 　　椎の花
Falling on the sidewalk 　　散る歩道
A sudden remembering 　　ふと
My hometown 　　わが故郷

Chapter11
Mao-sa-shi-no：Field of Linen Grass

十一章　苧種子野

Two Himalayan cedars	二本のヒマラヤ杉
Rose up to stand straight up	真直に立ち上がり
Only around them	そこのみは
Sense of woods	森林の
In the air	漂い
When we look up	見上げれば
Over swaying treetops	その梢揺らぐ果て
All the same	やはり森林の
Blue sky and	青空と
Clouds	雲

Waves of my destiny	運命の波
Let me go flow with you	流れゆくまゝに

In Musashino	武蔵野の
In the shadow of trees	木陰
Camellia flowers falling down	椿散るところ
Cherry blossoms falling down	桜散るところと
We walked on	歩きにけり

Sounds of wings	羽音
Passed us	よぎり
Tit birds	四十雀
Cry	鳴く

The spring sky	春の空
White	白き
The moon up	月
Gone through	雲より
Clouds	抜けてあり

Acacia flowers	ハリエンジュ
Bloom out	咲く
On the path along a stream	水流れゆく道
I walked with my wife	妻と歩きし

A rapid stream	急流
Falling down	落ちゆける
We picked up	木いちご
Raspberries	摘めり

Rapid streams	川瀬
Crashed to break	砕けゆく

Potherb mustard plants	水菜
We picked up at the stream	採りし沢
Only the clear water	清き水のみ
Streamed there	流れゆく

In loneliness	人去りて
An easter lily	鉄砲百合と
And me	我
Easter lily	鉄砲百合
Now	我去る
I am leaving	今も
Paulownia flowers	桐の花
Light purple	紫淡き
In my sorrow	わが愁い
They bloom shedding	五月の風に
Scents to May winds	咲き香る
High and blue the sky	高き青空
Under white clouds	白き雲の下
Sweet scabious flowers	姫紫苑
Grass of poverty	貧乏草と
Named someone	名づけられし
Sweet scabious flowers	姫紫苑
Bending to swing	止まりたる
With a butterfly	蝶と
Resting on	揺れたわむ

The butterfly	蝶
Fluttering	翻えり
Away	ゆく
Suddenly	急に
Cloudy	曇る
In the sky	空
Spring clouds	春の雲
Spring clouds	春の雲
Spring rain	春の雨
Sprays down	降る
Cloudy	曇り
Clears up	晴るゝ
The sky	空
Spring clouds	春の雲
Floats	ゆく
Spring clouds	春の雲
Bending through	窓
Windows	くぐり
To float there	ゆく

In a moment　　　　　　　　　　一瞬

A bird's shadow passing　　　　鳥影よぎり

When I look up　　　　　　　　見上げれば

Morning windows　　　　　　　朝の窓

Misty　　　　　　　　　　　　曇り

The path wet with dewdrops　　露の道

Lying on the bed　　　　　　　床にふす

I am　　　　　　　　　　　　我

Looking up　　　　　　　　　見ている

At a fluorescent lamp　　　　　蛍光灯

Just as when　　　　　　　　　幼き頃の

I was a boy　　　　　　　　　ま〻

This evening	今宵
A full moon	武蔵野の
In Musashino	満月
No blot at all	一点の曇りなき
When walking down	下りたてば
Backbones'	背骨の
Korean	朝鮮
Peninsula	再び
Flamed up again	火灯り
Musashino	武蔵野
Turns into	苧種子野と
Maosashino	なる
Fields of linen grass	

On this large earth	広き大地
I am serving	祭壇に
To the alter	仕える我
In Musashino	武蔵野に立つ
Smokes of Maosashino	苧種子野の煙
Fields of linen grass seeds	遠く
In a far distant	たなびく
Trailing	

Fire	われ
Pierced through	貫きて
Me	火
It is calm	静かなる
In Maosashino	苧種子野
In the spring	春
In Musashino	武蔵野の
The soil	土
I step on	我踏む
Gentle	足裏に
To my sole	優しき
In Maosashino	苧種子野
The soil	踏まれし
Stepped	土
In Maosashino	苧種子野の
The full moon	満月
Low	低く
Large	大きく
In a fire color	火の色
Yet again	帯びて
Turning dim	また
To go wane	幽か
	欠けてゆく

Croccus flowers	クロッカス
The flower bud	花蕾
In purple	紫の
A noble color	高貴なる
Thin	薄き
Flower stalks	花茎
Faint	幽かなる
In Maosashino	苧種子野

Croccus flowers	クロッカス
The flower	花
In the purple color	紫
Dark	濃く
Light	淡く
Becoming clearer	澄みゆく
In Maosashino	苧種子野

In Musashino	武蔵野の
Spring	春
The top of oak trees	楢こずえ
Light green	淡く
Dark green	濃く
Hastily sway	急ぎ揺る

Tit birds　　　　　　　四十雀

Calling　　　　　　　　春

The spring　　　　　　呼ぶ声

Twittering　　　　　　ツィーピツイピ

Twit-twit　　　　　　ツィーピと

I hear　　　　　　　　我

In Musashino　　　　武蔵野に

　　　　　　　　　　聞く

Again　　　　　　　　また

In Musashino　　　　武蔵野に

Snow falls　　　　　　雪降る

Far　　　　　　　　　遠く

Near　　　　　　　　近く

Lightly　　　　　　　春の

Spring snowfall　　　淡雪

The window　　　　　窓の

Full of dewdrops　　曇り

On it I draw　　　　まるく

A circle　　　　　　描き見る

To see　　　　　　　春の

Snow flakes　　　　　淡雪

In the spring

Hyacinth flowers	風信子
The flower buds	花蕾
Light purple	薄き紫に
On them	淡き雪
Light snow flakes fall	降る

Hyacinth flowers	風信子
Bloom out	咲く
In Musashino	武蔵野の
Fallen leaves	落葉
Now in silence	静かに

One	風信子
Hyacinth flower	一花の
The shadow	影
Faint	仄か

Daffodils	水仙
Grow up with no care	伸びやかに
In the early spring	春浅き
In Musashino Soil	武蔵野の
	土

Calla flowers   カラー

White   白き

Up to the heaven   花

Blooming out   天に向けて

                       咲く

Chapter12 Return

十二章　回帰

Croccus	クロッカス
Purple	紫の
Flowers	花
Pistils yellow	蕊黄
So bright	鮮やかに
In the depths	奥深き
White	白
Faintly	幽かなる
Amaryllis flowers	アマリリス
Scarlet color	深紅
The shadow deep	影深き
Doppo Kunikida	独歩を
When I see again	再び見れば
As I expect	やはり
I feel	苦しく
Painful	悲しいと
Sorrowful	思う
When I say	武蔵野と
Musashino	言えば
All the same	やはり
I think of	独歩を
Doppo	わが古里を
Of my hometown	少年の頃を
Of my boyhood	思う
I remember	

In the early spring	春浅き
In Musashino	武蔵野の
Water shadows	水影
Dim	幽か
Swaying	揺るゝ
Far	遠く
Near	近く
Shining	光り流れ
Flow to come	来る

The Sakurabashi Bridge	さくらばし
A little	武蔵野の
Clear water	清き水
Flows	わずか
In Musashino	たたうるに
In the stream	魚影
Fish shadow	一つ
One	静か
Drifting	漂いて
In silence	あり

In my life	生の
A new	新しき
Development	展開
Started with	それは
Sudden	不意の
Unexpected	思いがけない
Encounter with a girl	出会いによって
My sudden	始まる
Destiny	その突然の
In Musashino	運命と
	武蔵野

The God!	神
Why	何故
Do you express	世界を
The world?	表現する

I did	我
Why	何故
Come to the world?	世界に

Red cross

You left

Lonesome

Red plum blossoms

White ones

Blooming out on branches

Hanging down

Birds twittering across

Sasa veitchii leaves

Cypress leaves

The sun coming through trees

君去りし

赤十字

淋しかり

紅梅

白梅と

しだれ咲く

鳥鳴き渡り

熊笹葉群

桧葉

木洩れ日

Knowing

On my birth

On my continuing to exist

Is

As difficult as

Knowing

On God

この我の

成立と

存続の

いかにを

知ることは

神を

知るのと

同じ位

難しい

ことである

With me	我に
My father lives	父生き
My mother lights up	母灯りをり
In my hometown	我が古里に
My parents' hometown	父母の故郷
A windmill of	葦の葉の
Reed leaves	風車回りをり
Turning	
My Korea	我が朝鮮
I shall not have seen	見ることなく
To the end	終わる
When I see	我が古里の
Torch azalea flowers	山つつじ
In my hometown	見れば
I think of	父の故郷
My father's hometown	慶州の山
Where azalea flowers bloom	つゝじ思う
In mountains in Korea	

Balsam flowers	鳳仙花
Stalks and roots red	茎根赤く
Leaves transparent	葉透け
Flower shadows	花影
Dim	淡き
When they topple down	倒れれば
On the spot they grow	そこに根
Rooting	生う

Balsam flowers	鳳仙花
Becoming transparent	透けゆく
Beyond	時の
Time	彼方

Swaying	揺れる
Yellow daffodils	黄水仙
Innocent	あどけなき

Instantly	一瞬
A bulbul bird	ひよ鳥
Flew up	飛び立ちて
Sways	ゆれ
Left	のこる

On my lost	迷いし
Way	道
Magnolia kobus flowers	こぶし花
Bloom	咲く
Apricot flowers	杏花
Buds as they were	蕾のまゝに
Overflowed	こぼれ
Dropped	落つ
To see	見ること
To talk	語り
To be silent	黙ること
In an instant	一瞬
Breaking silence	突き破り
Piercing	ゆく
A cry	ひよ鳥の
Of a bulbul bird	声

The spring sky	春の空
Light	淡き
Blue	青
In a distant	遠く

My way I walked	来た道
So nostalgic	懐かし
When I turn back	振り返り
To see	見れば
The way	武蔵野
In Musashino	木洩れ日の
The sun leaks through trees	道

On a shore of the Tamagawa	上水べり
stream	山吹と
Japanese rose flowers	木いちご
Raspberry flowers	白き花
White flowers	咲きにけり
Bloomed out	

A way to go	ゆく道
A returning	回帰する
Way	道

Snowbell flowers	えごの花
In May winds	五月の風に
Fell down to carpet	散り敷く
In Musashino	武蔵野の
In the tree shadows	木陰
On the way	我歩きゆく道
I was walking	雉鳩の一羽
One turtledove	静かに
Silently	我を導きて
Led me	ゆけり
To go on	

Life	生は
Now	今すでに
Eternal	永遠である
What it means	その意味を
You can think more deeply but	深めこそすれ
You	それを
Cannot	くつがえす
Overturn	ことは
It	出来ない

On another shore of the good and	善悪の彼岸
evil	金木犀
Fragrant olive blossoms	香り来る
The scent coming over	

Where	われ
I bend myself	折る、ところ
In the mist	靄
Beyond	靄の
The mist	先
Further beyond is	その先の
Light	光
Where always	いつも
I stand still	佇む所
Now	今
Magnolia kobus blossoms	こぶし花
Bloom	咲く
In dry grass	枯草の中
Apricot flowers	杏花
Opened	咲けり

In Musashino	武蔵野の
Unexpected for me	思わず
Wheat fields	麦畑の
Spreading	広がり
The ears	穂群
In winds	風に
Waving	波打ち
Swaying	揺る、
My eyes	我が目
My mind	わが心
Sway together	共に揺る
Light shall	光
Come to reach	届き来る
The place where	わが命
I am living	あるところ
You	君
Return home	帰り来る
Your step sounds	足音
In my pulsation	我が鼓動

Final Chapter FLOWER SHADOW

終章　花の影

Reading	書に
A book when	目を落とし
A bird's shadow	居ると
In a moment	鳥影
Passed away	一瞬
	よぎる

Raising up my eyes	目を上げ
I follow	その影
The shadow	追えど
I can not see	その影
It	再び
Again	見えず

G. Lange	ランゲ
"Flower Song"	花の歌

Flower shadow	花の影
The shadow	永遠なるものゝ
Something eternal	影

White plum flower	白梅一輪
Hanging down	しだるゝまゝに
Touches me	我に触れ
Swaying	揺る

Chcrry blossoms	桜
In the blizzard	吹雪く

At my foot	わが
Petals of cherry blossoms	足元に
Whirling	桜花びら
Together	うずまき
Go racing	そろいて
	走る

On the back of a leaf of cherry trees	桜葉に
A cicada	蟬
Stopping	さかさまに
Upside down	止まりいる
In the summer afternoon	夏の午後

Twining	葛藤の
Kudzu vines	葛
The flower shadow	花影
Calm	静かなる

Last night	昨夜の
The storm wild	嵐
This morning	今朝
Weigela flowers	源平うつぎ
Scattered	散りをり

White powder flowers	白粉花
Opened and withered	咲き
In the morning	しぼみし朝
I awoke	我
	目覚めり
Camellia buds	椿莟
Still tight	まだ堅き
For	暮れに
The end of a year	向けて
Still	我
I am alive	なお
	生きてをり
When I was young	かの昔
In the spring storm	春嵐に
Apricot blossoms	杏花
Still as buds	莟のまゝに
Dropped down to scatter	こぼれ散り
Camellia flowers	椿花
Harshly	激しく
Swinging	揺るゝ日
On the day I remember	ありし
Spring storm	春の嵐
When it is violent	激しければ
Resembles the sounds	わが悔いの
In my regrets	音にも似たり

The more I regret	悔いる程に
The more calm	わが魂の
The more peaceful	静まり
My soul feels	安まるなり

At my foot	わが
My own shadow	足元の
Burying	わが影
Snow	埋ずみ
Falling on	雪
	降りしきる

A swallow	つばめ
Flutters	翻えり
To hover	静止する
In the air	一瞬
The moment	

A black butterfly	黒き蝶
Fluttering	翻えり
Some time	ふと
Gone out of my sight	消えぬ

What	我
I saw	見しもの
what is seen	見えしもの

What	神
God	我に
Showed me	見せしもの
In the world and	世界と
In my mind	我の
	なかに
Up to the heaven	天上への
Each time for me	その都度の
One by one	一点一点の
Points and lines	点と線
To God	神に
I wish to come closer	接しゆく
With my words	自己本来より
Welling up	湧き出づる
From my proper self	言葉

Time	時は
Passing away	過ぎ去り
Coming to the end	終りつつ
In the course	その都度の
In each moment called now	今一瞬のなかで
To beyond time	時の彼方へと
Time leads	われを
Me	導く

I will turn to	我がそれであるところの
What I am	自己本来であるところのものに
What my proper self is	なる

Be proper myself	自己本来の永遠的存在であれ
In the eternal existence	と言う

Oh my death!	死よ
Inevitable	さけがたく
Coming along close to my life	わが生にそい来る
Darkness	暗き闇
While there is light	光あるうちに
Shrouding my life	わが生を包み
Carry me away	永遠なるものへと
Into the eternal	運び去れよ

Even now	今すでに
On my grave	わが墓の上に
Pine winds rustle	松風鳴り
Bunting birds twitter	頬白さえずり
Under grass	下草に
Bellflowers	桔梗花
Swing	揺る

Steams up from hot springs	湯けむりの
Rising up in a cloud	雲わきあがる
In a winter grove	冬木立

In the grove full of steams	湯けむりの木立
Red cheeked	赤き頬の
A bird	鳥
Resting	止まりをり

Running the steams	湯けむり走る
Ripples of the hot spring	湯さざなみ

In the hot steam	湯けむりの
A full moon	満月
A rainbow	虹
Hanging	架かりをり

The water going?　　　　　ゆく水か

The water coming?　　　　　来る水か

In my traveling inn　　　　旅の宿

While I am　　　　　　　　我

Sleeping　　　　　　　　　眠る間も

Restless　　　　　　　　　休みなく

The stream babbling　　　　せせらぎ

Runs on　　　　　　　　　流る

Climbed to the end　　　　登りつめし

On the way　　　　　　　　道

Plum blossoms fragrant　　梅香る

A stone image of Buddha　　石仏

When looking up　　　　　見上げれば

Kite birds　　　　　　　　トンビ

Melting into clouds　　　　雲にまじりて

Flying　　　　　　　　　　飛ぶ

High and　　　　　　　　　高く

Low　　　　　　　　　　　低く

Coming and going　　　　　行き交う

Clouds　　　　　　　　　　雲あり

In Kimigahama coast	君ヶ浜
What I lost	失われしもの
Piling up	積み重なりて
Endlessly	果てなく
Spreading	続き
With no borders	境なく
Disappeare	消ゆる

A lighthouse	灯台
White	白く
The cliff	断崖
Falls into the sea	海に落つ

In the sea	海
Where	一きわ
The bluest in the color	青きところ
Seagulls	カモメ
Flying in a flock	群れとぶ

When it is cloudy	曇りたれば
Seagulls	カモメ
Fly to clouds	雲にとぶ

Seagulls   カモメ
Folding wings   羽根たたみ
Drifting   波間に
Between waves   漂う

Only with withered grass   枯草のみの
On the hill top   海の
In a view of the sea   丘

In an empty house   廃屋に
Vine bellflower   つる桔梗
In bloom   咲く

A driftwood   流木の
The skin smooth   肌すべらかに
Sea breezes blow   海風の吹く

A driftwood   流木の肌
The skin   白く
Weathered into white   さらばえて
Lies to rest   休めり

A driftwood	流木の肌
The skin	白く
White	すべらかに
Smoothly	さらばえて
Weathered	海風に
In the sea breeze	休めり
Resting	

A stone	わが
At my foot	足元の
Weathered	石は
To inscribe	風化して
Time	時を
	刻めり

Only	神が
The time	与えし
God	時
Gave	のみを

In Kimigahama coast	君ヶ浜
What I lost	失われしもの
Piles up	積み重なりて
Endlessly	果てなく
Spreading	続く
Evening primroses	月見草

Wave crests rise up	波頭たつ
The sea in a distant	遠き海
I hear	音することも
No sounds	なく

Barely left	わずかに
The sands	残る砂
Scarcely visible	かすかなる
Footprints	足跡

With my wife	妻と
I walked	歩き
I parted from her	別れし
The sea	海
Shines	光る

Crinum lilies	浜ゆう
Blooming	咲く

A crinum lily	浜ゆう
A crinum lily	はまゆう
Blooming	咲く

A Crinum lily	浜ゆう
Never forgets	忘れず
Crinum lily	はまゆう
In bloom	咲く

Depths	無限の
Infinite	奥ゆき
Looking up to the heaven	天上見れど
Looking down at my foot	足元見れど
The depths of my life	わが生の奥
The further depth much deeper	またその奥
When I see	見れど

On a treetop	遠く
Far and	高き
High up	梢
A cry of a cuckoo	カッコー
Echoing	木霊して
Goes vanish	消えてゆく

Nature's	自然の
Endless	無限の
Abyss	奥

On a lcaf	里芋の
Of a taro potato	葉
Slanting though	斜めなりに
A dewdrop	露

One dewdrop	一露
On a leaf of a taro potato	里芋の葉
In a sway	揺り
Dropped down	落つ

A leaf	里芋の
Of a taro potato	葉
A swaying	揺るゝ
Part	別れ

A mountain pigeon	山鳩
Alone goes	一羽
Flying away	とび去りゆく

Opera	カヴァレリア
Cavalleria Rusticana	ルスチカーナ
Comes into my hearing	聞こえ来る

Water lilies bloom	睡蓮咲く
On the water surface	水面に
Reflects	映る
The blue sky	高き
High and clouds	青空と雲

On all daily affairs	すべてのことに
Voices of sorrow	悲しみの声
I hear	聞こゆ
Though	されど
I listen to them again	また聞けば
On all these things	すべてのことに
Voices of joy	喜びの声
I can hear	聞こえ来る
God	神我に
Gave me	すべてのことを
All	与えけり
Voices of	悲しみと
Sorrows and Joys	喜びの声なり

Into a flower	花の中
A butterfly	蝶一つ
Entering and	入りて
Going	出でて
Out	ゆく

When I look up	見上げれば
Dazzling	目まう
A bird shadow	鳥の影
One cloud	雲一つ
Flowing	ゆく
In the direction	方に
Wheat grass	麦草の
In a large field	広がり
Their ears	穂群
In the wind	風に
Waving	波打ち
Sway	揺るゝ
In the late autumn	晩秋の
The setting sun	夕日
Wanting to see more	惜しみ
On a hill	丘に
I go up climbing	登りゆく

A red dragonfly	赤トンボ
On my chest	我が胸に
Stopping	止まり
Its wings	羽根
Take a rest	安めをり

A red dragonfly	赤トンボ
As life	命
So light	軽やかに
Flew away	飛び去りに
From me	けり

A blue sky	青空
The blue color	青
Beyond	無限の
Infinity	彼方

A half moon	半月
White	白く
Floats up	浮かびをり

When I gaze	見つむれば
White	白き
Ears of grass	草の穂
Faintly	かすか
Sway	揺れてをり

The setting sun	夕日
On water surface	水面に
Reflecting	反射し
To my eyes and	わが目と
To my soul	魂に
Shines	燦然と
Bright	輝く

My life	わが生の
Reached	辿り着きし
The eternal	永遠なる
Present	今

Light	光
Comes over	及び来る
At my foot	わが
On the water shore	足元の
Rush grasses	水辺
Sway in the breeze	灯心草
	そよぐ

The Collected Poems *MUSASHINO* – On Destiny and Return

1
On my poetry book *MAOSASHINO* : Field of Linen Grass

When I knew about "Maosashio:A Field of Linen Grass," around at the ending time, when I was editing my poetry book of *MUSASHINO*.

When *MUSASHINO* suddenly turned into *Maosashino*: A Field of Linen Grass.

At the time, through a research book, I knew the word root of "MUSASHINO" was words in Korean language.

According to the book, the author said, "Maosashino" means "a field of some kind of linen grass seeds" which immigrants from Korea brought and planted in the district now so-called, around the age of 600 A.D..

When I knew it, I felt the deepest emotions beyond words.

Returning home with the book in my hand, I got off the train and stood at the station of Musashi-sakai, when I looked a full moon up in the sky, there.

It was a most brilliant moon, I ever saw.

The moon was up in the sky of Musashino area, low and so big with fire color.

The poem I made immediately on the spot was," This evening/ A full moon/ In Musashino/ No blot at all/ When walking down/ Back bones'/ Korean/ Peninsula/ Flamed up again/ Musashino/ Turns into/ Maosashino/ A Field of Linen Grass"

One of the deep emotions I felt then was in a memory that a literary novel in Japan, *Musashino* by Doppo Kunikida, a Japanese novelist, awakened me to literature.

I was born and grew up in a village, in Ibaraki prefecture. At that time I was a boy student of a middle high school.

It was over forty years ago, from now.

Then, I did not know which district was "Musashino," and I had never thought of it.

But later, I realized that I was living in the district myself, and edited my poetry book *MUSASHINO*.

In addition, in the depths of my emotions, there was a fact that I grew up as a Korean resident in Japan in the second generation.

And, because my hometown in Japan, and the nature in Ibaraki, resembled that of Musashino area, as the result I found a coincidence of my nostalgic "Musashino" and my birth place. It was unexpected and so strange. （December 20, 2002)

To me, at the time, it was so impressive that I knew the word root of "Musashino" was in Korean language.

And, a full moon large and brilliant welcomed me when I descended to stand up before the station of Musashi-sakai. It was unexpectedly when I wrote in my poem," Musashino/ turns into/ Maosashino/A field of linen grass"

It happened on February 11, in 1998.

But, on the next day, in the evening, the full moon "Yet again/ Turning dim/ To go wane"

And, the "Maosashino," shifting calmly in my mind,

Goes to "Fire/ Pierced through/ Me/ It is calm/ In Maosashino"

Then into "On this large earth/ I am serving/ To the alter/ In Musashino/ Smokes of Maosashino/ Fields of linen grass seeds/ In a far distant /

Trailing"

Again into "A way to go/ A return way," I feel as if these poems of mine had a premonition of my way in the future and talked of it.

They say books have fates. I wonder if my books by themselves could feel and talk on their own fates.

Or, does God talks through the author, turning himself into the soul of books, and becoming the words, to tell us our destiny?

The author and his books, are led by God, by his destiny?

Indeed now, it is strange that writing it, I feel like I am led by God, by my destiny, myself not knowing how the hand of God works.

2
Walking in Musashino

In Musashino area I used to walk. First, around the Musashino Hospital, which had the nursing school Yoko attended, secondly, beside the clear stream, close to Musashi-sakai Station.

Going the way up a bit, we can see Sakurabashi Bridge, ahead the bridge, the stream continued long to the Tama River, the stream source.

We walked in the area as far as we could, and returned to Mitaka Station.

Getting off a train at Mitaka Station, and we changed trains for more one station, to Musashi-sakai, and we returned home.

In addition, I frequented to walk around Tsutsujigaoka, in Chofu.

It was the first place in Musashino, for me, where once, I lived with my first wife, after we got married.

It was for four years, from my age of twenty three to twenty seven.

In my poems, when I wrote as a wife, she means the lady at the time.

It passed thirty years, When I started to live with Yoko, in the live oak's lodge.

Later, after many years, I again came to live in the Musashino area, Mu-sashi-sakai where I met Yoko, was my second Musashino area to live.

In Tsutsujigaoka at that time, I started a new life and I had a family. It seemed that I was liberated from my severe and lonely life, at last.

And I started walking around to trail in the nature of the Musashino area. The nature of Musashino area resembled that of my hometown, in Ibara-ki. Feeling nostalgic to my birth place, I was walking around the area. And, while I walked on repeatedly, I was having new discoveries on the nature reaching the depths.

The sense of nature I was awakened in the course, turned into something romantic and pantheistic, in myself, to be deepened and to be ripened.

My poetic mind to nature, in addition to that of Doppo Kunikida, started linking to English romanticism, whose representative is Wordsworth, and to the spirit of German romanticism, so-called "Gemuetich", which put values on our living in nature with joys and admires. I called to nature, "Oh!/ Thou!/ Woods!/ Nature!" and as if intoxicated, I even called out," My life is/ To deepen/ That oak treetop," So much I praised nature.

My sense of nature, which was awakened by *MUSASHINO*, written by a Japanese novelist Doppo Kunikida, in my young days. It led me then to the idea, "to see God in the beauty of nature and its order."

My experiences in Nature at the time, later, led me to more important significance.

My life in Tsutsujigaoka, at the time, had such a profound meaning, which stayed deep in my mind.

I called those days as my Tsutsujigaoka times, and thought it to be so important in my life.

When in the woods of poplar trees, I was walking on the way, upon which an azure-winged magpie bird flew across, I saw unexpectedly wheat fields spreading. I sang that "In Musashino/ Unexpectedly/ Spreading/Wheat ears/ In the winds/ Waving/ Swaying/ My eyes/ My mind/ Together sway." This poem was a memory then.

My poems which I again visited and I trailed the ways I walked decades ago were, "That treetop/ Sky/ Even now/ There/ In Musashino/ A narrow path/ I trail/ I trailed.," "In Musashino/ The way nostalgic/ When I go trailing/ Akebia flowers/ Five-cluster leaves/ Not falling down,/ and, "Wolfberries/ Barely/ Left." As representing the time flowing, and just as being in solitude, the poem continues. "By the shrine/ A tree/ Ginkgo leaves/ Falling on/ A way/ in Musashino"

Again I trailed the way, which decades ago I had walked on. Just as I had done once, I stood on the same way, and I saw the same sky and a treetop. And, as decades ago, Akebia blossoms barely not falling down and go-jiberry were very few of them left.

Leaves of the ginkgo tree, beside the roadside, was falling on.

" In musashino/ A narrow road in my memory/ Climbing to come/ looking back/ My empty past/ In the setting sun/ Melting into clouds/ Like in blood/ The evening smoke was trailing around" was that, when I climbed the way again I once frequently climbed, that day climbing up and looked back my past around the place where I had lived, the setting sun, like blood, melting into clouds and only the evening smoke was trailing around.

The area in which I once lives was around the shore of the Irumagawa River, where Tsutsujigaoka hill spreading right and left, continuing to the Senkawa River and to the hills around Jindaiji Temple.

It was thirty yeas ago since I visited there from the oak's lodge. Since then it passed twenty five yeas. So, counting totally from now, it was fifty five years ago.

At the time, I frequently listened to Chopin's Piano Concerto and Tchaikovsky's Symphony, "Pathetique." They, even now resound in my heart. And all of my life in Tsutsujigaoka invited me into the romantic and pathetic feeling, and then, leaving all of them in a kind of nothingness, they gone vanishing away.

Why I returned to Tsutsujigaoka and trailed back repeatedly the ways I had walked, is, because though I experienced my failures and losses after I left there, I had a nostalgia to my days in Tsutsujigaoka, I think.

The area was also connecting to my nostalgia to the nature of my hometown. And, just like the expression of nature in Doppo's novel *MUSASHINO*, I saw there in musashino, from treetops of decidous trees, on a small hill, red leaves whirled up and down, blown by harsh winds.

It was the Doppo's *MUSASHINO*, which I read in my young days, and gave me a great emotion, when it came to the expression that red leaves whirled by winds, from the deciduous treetops in the late autumn.

Thus, my walking in Musashino area, started from the oak's lodge, then to the clear stream in Mitaka, and lastly to Tsutsujigaoka. It trailed back my pilgrimages to the past.

But, those walks were not ended only in my nostalgia to my hometown, and not in my recollections to my past. Including my walks in Tsutsujigaoka, I was in just the course of my growing up, in my new discovers on nature and deepening them in my mind...

3

Monument For Kunikida Doppo

On the day, when I happened to feel lonliness I went out with Yoko, to walk along the clear water stream.

We got out of the live oak's lodge and walked a little along the stream shore, suddenly, I found out a monument for Doppo Kunikida.

It was unexpected happening to me.

I walked the way with Yoko, so many times, but I did not notice the monument.

It stood there, on the shore of the clear water stream, quiet and calm, in the sunlight leaking down through trees in Musashino in the beginning of summer.

I felt like it had been waiting for our arrival.

I stood still before the monument with Yoko, for some time, with a great impression.

My memories came up to me, turning like a revolving lantern: that I read his novel, *MUSASHINO* by Doppo. That, as if led by my destiny, I moved to live in the Musashino area. That in the Musashino area, I met Yoko. And lastly that I came to write my poetry book, titled in *MUSASHINO*. It was a far and long way.

I remembered my poem, "A far way/ Detouring/ Crossing/ And returning" If it was led by God, it would have been in my destiny, set, at least since I was born to this world. If it was led by the spirit of Doppo, it would have been set by him, since the day when he passed away.

4
Aniversary Day of Doppo's Passing

My publication of MULBERRIES was just on the same day with Yoko's birthday. On a day when her birthday was approaching close, I happened to check Doppo's biography and my eyes stopped on the notation of his anniversary day for his passing.

It was on the same day with Yoko's birthday, June 23.

It was also so much astonishing to me.

For a moment, I doubted my sight.

Since I met Yoko, I celebrated some birthdays of hers, including her birthday of twenty years old, for the first time. But I did not know the day was the same day with the Doppo's anniversary day for passing.

Yoko was born on the very day of the anniversary day for Doppo's passing.

I wondered if it was only an unexpected happening.

Could I say that this discovery and a series of other things were all supposed to be mere results of coincidences?

Who can say that, originally we had no God or no God's providence. And all happenings, in my destiny, were mere series of accidents with no purposes nor any significance?

What on the earth, was Musashino to me?

I was living my life since I was born, as Korean resident in Japan. Holding worries and conflicts, which are beyond my expression. I lived feeling myself as if a child of wondering immigrants.

Choson, now called Korea, which my parents told me, seemed me like a hometown in a distant and in an illusion. It did not seem like a country to me. Korea, the new name, was unfamiliar and strange to me.

However, I could have never become a Japanese, in my mind. I grew up feeling some strangeness to Japanese manners and cultures.

But, eventually, the problems came to be solved out in the Musashino area.

It was because of my publication of my poetry book *MUSASHINO*, in my destiny and in my encounter with a lady in the area, that I could carry out my self-establishment as well as my self-transcendence.

What do they mean, the self-establishment and the self-transcendence?

I think that they shall become clearer to you, in the course of your reading my poems in *MUSASHINO*. They show by themselves up to you, in the course of my realization: to fulfill my own proper identity, to cross over borders of races and countries, to jump over my narrow consciousness as a Korean resident in Japan, and, getting aware of myself as one member of humankind, I will live as a universal man in the world.

Note: Doppo Kunikida (1871-1908), a Japanese novelist, poet. *MUSASHINO* is one of his famous novels. He was once living in Kichi-joji, in the Musashino area.

詩集『武蔵野』運命と回帰

1
詩集『苧種子野』について

　私が苧種子野について知ったのは、詩集『武蔵野』を編集していた最後の頃であった。

　そこで『武蔵野』は突然『苧種子野』となったのであった。

　その時私は、ある研究書によって、武蔵野の語源が朝鮮語であることを知った。

　それによると、紀元六〇〇年代頃の朝鮮からの渡来人が、今の武蔵野の地域に、織物の技術と共に持ち来たった麻の一種、「苧の種子」の野という意味によるものとあった。

　それを知った私は、胸中深く幾重にも、言い知れぬ感動を覚えるのであった。

　その書を手に帰途、武蔵境駅に降り立つと、折しも武蔵野は満月であった。

　それは今までに見たこともないほどの、実に見事なものであった。

　月は、低く大きく火の色を帯びて、武蔵野の空に掛かるのであった。

　その時その場で成った詩が「今宵　武蔵野の　満月　一点の曇りなき　下りたてば　背骨の　朝鮮　再び　火灯り　武蔵野　苧種子野となる」である。

　その胸中幾重もの感動の一つは、私の文学の目覚めが独歩の『武蔵野』であったことである。

　私は茨城県の山村で生まれ育ち、当時中学生の少年であった。

　今から四十数年も前に遡る頃である。

　その時私は、武蔵野がどの地域の地名なのか知らず、また考えてみ

ることもなかった。

それが後年、いつの間にか気がついてみると、自らがその地に住み、そして詩集『武蔵野』を著しているのであった。

さらに次の感動の深層は、私自身、在日朝鮮人二世としての生い立ちを持っていることであった。

そして、日本での私の故郷、その地の自然が、武蔵野の自然に似ていることもあり、わが郷愁の武蔵野と自分自身のルーツが、思いがけず奇しくも符合するところとなったのである。（二〇〇二年十二月二十日）

当時の私にとって、武蔵野の語源が朝鮮語であることを知ったことは、実にそれ程に感動的なことであった。

そして武蔵境駅前に下り立った私を迎えた武蔵野の空に掛かる見事な満月、その光景は、思いがけず、「武蔵野 苧種子野と なる」瞬間となったのである。

一九九八年二月十一日の夕のことであった。

しかし、その満月は、翌日の夕には「また 幽か 欠けてゆく」のであった。

そして「苧種子野」は、わが胸中に穏やかに推移しつつ、「われ貫きて 火 静かなる 苧種子野」と続き、「広き大地 祭壇に 仕える我 武蔵野に立つ 苧種子野の煙 遠く たなびく」とあり、「遠き道 迂回し 交叉し 回帰する」とあり、「来た道 懐かし 振り返り 見れば 武蔵野 木洩れ日の 道」とあり、再び「行く道 回帰する 道」とあり、自らのこれから先の運命の道筋を予感し語っているかのようである。

本には運命がある、と言われるが、本自らが自らの運命を予感し語る、と言うこともあるのだろうか。

あるいは神が作者を通し、本の魂となり、言葉となり、運命を語るのであろうか。

それによって、作者も、本も、自ずとその運命によって、神に導かれてゆくのであろうか。

　今現に、このように書いている私も、何やら我知らず、運命によって、神に導かれ書いているような感じがするのは、不思議なことである。

2
武蔵野歩行

　私がよく散策した武蔵野は、まずは、樫の宿周辺で、容子が通っていた看護大学があった武蔵野病院のあたりと、武蔵境近くの上水べりであった。

　そこの上水べりを少し行くと、さくらばしがあり、その先は延々と源流の多摩川にまで続いているのであった。

　そこを行ける所まで行って、三鷹まで戻り、三鷹から下り電車で一駅乗って、武蔵境へと帰途につくのであった。

　それからまた更に、故あって、調布市のつつじヶ丘周辺によく出かけ、歩いたのであった。

　つつじヶ丘は、昔、私が結婚当初住んだ、最初の武蔵野の地であったのである。

　二十三から二十七歳までの四年間のことであった。

　詩集中、妻とあるは、その時のその人のことである。

　樫の宿の容子との生活より、三十年前のことである。

　その後、後年に至り、再び武蔵野の地に住むこととなり、容子と出会った武蔵野は、私にとって二度目の武蔵野であったのである。

　私は、当時つつじヶ丘での新しい生活の中で、家庭を持ち、それまでの厳しい孤独な生活から、ようやく解放されたようであった。

　そして、付近の武蔵野の自然を辿り、歩行するようになったのであ

る。

　武蔵野の自然が古里の自然と似通っていたこともあり、古里への郷愁の念と共に、武蔵野の自然と思しきところを辿り、繰り返し歩行するうちに、新たな自然の発見と深まりに達して行ったのである。

　その中で目覚めた自然観は、ロマン主義的、汎神論的なものとなって深まり、熟成されたのである。

　私の自然に対する詩的心情は、独歩の自然観に加え、ワーズワスを初めとする、イギリスロマン主義と、ドイツロマン主義の心情、ゲミュートも加わり、「汝　林よ　自然よ」と呼びかけ、陶酔し、「私の人生は　あの楢の梢を　深めることに過ぎない」とまで言い放って、自然を謳歌したのである。

　少年の頃に、独歩の『武蔵野』によって目覚めた自然観は、ここに至って、「自然の美と　秩序に　神を見る」と言うところまでに達したのである。

　この時期の自然体験は、後に至って、なお一層重要な意味を持つようになるのである。

　当時のつつじヶ丘での生活は、それ程に意味深く、胸中深く宿っていたのであった。

　私は、その頃を、つつじヶ丘時代と呼び、終生大事に思っていたのである。

　ポプラの林を尾長が渡りゆく下道を行く私の目の前に、思いがけず広がる麦畑を、「武蔵野の　思わず　麦畑の　広がり　穂群　風に波打ち　揺る、　我が目　わが心　共に揺る」と歌ったのは、その時の思い出からのものである。

　つつじヶ丘を再び訪れ、昔歩行した道を、また辿り歩く中で書かれた詩篇は、「かの　梢　空　今もあり　武蔵野の　小道　我辿る　辿りし道」とあり、「武蔵野の　懐かしき道　辿りゆけば　木通　五つ葉の　散りやらず」とあり、「枸杞の実　わずか　残りし」と、時の移

り行きを表わすように淋しく続き、「祠木の　銀杏　散るなり　武蔵野の　道」とある。

　昔歩いたその道を、また辿り歩き、昔そうしたように、同じ所に佇み見れば、同じ空と梢ありしが、木通の五つ葉は、辛うじて散りやらず、枸杞の実も、わずかに残るばかりであった。

　道端の小さな祠のそばにある銀杏の木の葉は、晩秋の道に淋しく散るばかりであった。

「武蔵野の　思い出の細き小道　登り来て　振り返り見れば　わが空しき過去　落日　血のごとく雲にとけ　夕の煙たなびきてをり」とあるは、昔良くその道を歩き登った懐かしい道、今再び登り来て、振り返り見れば、わが空しき過去、我かつて住みしあたり、落日、血のごとく雲にとけ、夕の煙たなびきてをり、とただあるばかりである。

　我かつて住みしあたりとは、入間川のほとり、つつじヶ丘が、左右に、仙川の、そして深大寺の周辺の丘陵にと続くところであった。

　それは、私が、樫の宿からそこを訪れたその時より、三十年前のことであり、その後また、更に二十五年たった今からすれば、五十五年前のことである。

　当時良く聴いていた、ショパンのピアノ協奏曲と、チャイコフスキーの交響曲、悲愴が、今もわが胸中に鳴り、つつじヶ丘の全てのことを、ロマンと悲愴の中へと誘い、そしてまた、その全てを、虚無の中へと置き去りにして、消えてゆくのである。

　私が、またつつじヶ丘を訪ね、昔歩行した道を、くりかえし辿り歩くようになったことには、その後の人生の挫折と喪失と、かつてのつつじヶ丘時代へのノスタルジアがあったことによると思われる。

　つつじヶ丘は、また、私の古里の自然への郷愁にもつながり、そして更に独歩の『武蔵野』の自然の描写にあるように、小高い丘の落葉樹の梢から、一陣の風に、紅葉が舞い下りるところでもあったのである。

それは、かつて少年の頃読んだ独歩の『武蔵野』が、晩秋の落葉樹の梢から、紅葉がいっせいに風に散り舞うところの描写に至った時、当時少年であった私の胸中に、言い知れぬ感慨が生じたところであった。

　それが、私の文学の目覚めと共に自然観の目覚めとなったのである。

　かくして、武蔵野歩行は、樫の宿から上水べりを経て、つつじヶ丘に至り、私の過去への心の遍歴を辿るのである。

　しかし、その歩行は、単に古里への、そして過去へのノスタルジアと回想に終わるものではなく、つつじヶ丘時代の歩行もそうであったように、常に新たな自然の発見と深化と共に、人生の熟成の中にあったものと思われる。

　3
　独歩の文学碑

　その日ふと淋しさを覚えた私は、容子と連れ立って、上水べりへと散歩に出かけたのであった。

　樫の宿から歩いて、上水べりを少し行くと、ふと目に止まったのは、独歩の文学碑であった。

　それは思いがけないことであった。

　その道は、容子と一緒に何度も歩いた道であったが、そこに独歩の文学碑があることに気付かなかったのである。

　それは、武蔵野の初夏の木洩れ日の中に、静かにひっそりとした佇まいで、上水の水のせせらぎの辺に立っていたのであった。

　それは、あたかも、その日の私達の到来を待って居てくれたかのような感じがするものであった。

　私は、容子と共にそこに暫し佇み、深い感慨に浸るのであった。

　少年の頃に出会った、独歩の『武蔵野』、後に、運命に導かれるよ

うに移り住むこととなった武蔵野の地、そこでの容子との出会い、そして詩集『武蔵野』を書くことになったこと等、走馬灯のごとく巡るのであった。

　思えば、遠い道程であった。

「遠き道　迂回し　交叉し　回帰する」の詩篇が、胸中また去来するのであった。

　それが神の計らいによるものであったならば、それは永遠の昔からの定めであり、少なくとも、私がこの世に生を受け、誕生した時からのものであり、もし独歩の魂の導きによるものと言うならば、独歩の没年の時からのものであろうと思われるのである。

　　4
　　独歩の命日

『桑の実』の出版が、丁度折良く容子の誕生日と重なり、その日を間近に控えたある日のこと、私は、何げなく独歩の伝記を見ていたのであるが、独歩の命日にさしかかった時、思わずその日付に、私の目が止まったのである。

　それは、容子の誕生日と同じ、六月二十三日であったのである。

　これには、私はまた相当に驚いたのであった。

　一瞬、わが目を疑った程であった。

　容子と出会って以来、彼女の二十歳の誕生日を初めとして、何度も彼女の誕生日を迎えたのであるが、それが独歩の命日であることは知らなかったのである。

　容子は、独歩の命日に誕生した人であったのである。

　これが、単なる偶然と言って済まされることであろうか。

　この事が、そしてその他の一連のことが、全て、単なる偶然の羅列の結果に過ぎないと言えるであろうか。

元より、神もなければ、神の摂理というものはなく、全ては、運命は、単なる偶然の連続であり、意味も目的もないものと、誰が言えるであろうか。

　武蔵野とは、一体私にとって何であったのだろうか。

　私は幼い時から在日としての出自の故に、言い知れぬ苦悩と葛藤を抱え込み、流浪の民の子のように生きていたのである。

　両親が語る祖国朝鮮は、遠くまぼろしの中の故郷のことであり、国を成しておらず、その後の韓国と言う言葉も、なじみのない、違和感のあるものであった。

　と言って、決して内心からは日本人には成り切れず、日本の風俗文化にもなじめないものを感じながら育ったのである。

　それが、最終的に、武蔵野の地で、その解決が果たされることになったのである。

　それは、その地での運命と出会いの中で、詩集『武蔵野』を著すことで、自己確立と自己超越を果たすことによって遂げることが出来たのであった。

　自己確立と自己超越とは、何を言うのであろうか。

　それは詩集『武蔵野』を辿りゆけば、それが指し示す方向に、自ずから見えて来るものであると思われるが、本来の自己を全うし、民族と国家との壁を越え、在日としての自らの意識の狭い壁を越え、自らを人類の一員として自覚し、普遍的人間として生きてゆく方向に指し示されようとするものと思われるのである。

注：国木田独歩（1871-1908）日本の小説家、詩人。武蔵野市吉祥寺に住んだ。小説『武蔵野』は代表作のひとつである。

Commentary

解説

Commentary

3,000 lines of lyrical and ontological contemplative poems about Musashino, the old countryside

"The Collected Poems of Toshiaki An in English & Japanese *MUSASHINO*"
(translated by Noriko Mizusaki)

Hisao Suzuki

1

In "Musashino/武蔵野" by Toshiaki An, lines of mainly short poems of three to seven lines each are piled up as a suite of poems. As you begin to read, you are drawn into the rhythmic sense of stream of consciousness of the here and now. Before you know it, images of men and women living in "Musashino" and numerous plants and birds appear, and you are reminded of the depths and ancient layers of our memories, like a sense of déjà vu. We feel a mysterious and fertile experience that somehow connects the depths of our memories with those of Mr. An's. Mr. An's psalms are not the same as those of forgotten memories, but rather, they are a reflection of our own. His psalms are like Bach's suite of 3,000 lines of unaccompanied cello music that recalls the memory of Musashino, the ancient home where our diverse ancestors once lived and worked, and which responds to our inner supple sensibility. At the same time, while it is a lyric poem, it also contains an ontological question, a raw contemplation.

"Musashino" means the field of "Musashi." "Musashi" was first mentioned in history books in the 530s in the Nihon shoki (Chronicles of Japan) as "Musashinokuni no Miyakko no Ran (Rebellion of Musashi Province)." At that time, it was also called "Muzashi/无邪志" but later, in the 7th century, the name was unified into "Musashi," the name of the region in Chinese characters, and was officially recorded. "Kuninomiyakko" refers to "hereditary local government officials before the Taika Reform," but the extent of their authority is still a mystery. In the history of the area, there was a "rebellion" in which the Yamato Imperial Court intervened in the internal disputes of a powerful clan. The area is said to have pointed to the central part of the Kanto Plain, which spanned from the Tama River to the Ara River and included Kanagawa, Tokyo, and Saitama. The "Musashino Line," which is derived from the word "Musashino," once ran through the wilderness from Chiba Prefecture, where I live, through Saitama Prefecture to Fuchu in Tokyo, but now runs through suburban bedroom towns and continues to encircle the center of Tokyo.

It is likely that a large number of people from the Korean Peninsula arrived in this "Musashino" around the 6th century A.D., bringing with them a variety of technologies. The memories of the Koguryo people are engraved in "Komae" in present-day Tokyo and "Korai-gun, Saitama Prefecture". As if called by these memories, An published his first collection of poems, "苧種子野(Musashino)/" in 2002, followed by a collection of poems, "Mulberry Fruits" in 2005. Based on those two books, twenty years later, in 2022, he published a collection of poems, Musashino (Japanese edition). It is said that an essential poet lives to leave only one collection of poems in his lifetime. It seems as if Mr. An lived his life to preserve this collection of poems, Musashino. In the afterword to his poetry collection "Musashino," Mr. An wrote, "According to a research book, the word Musashino comes from a Korean word meaning "ramie/苧 field," a type of hemp that was brought to Japan with weaving techniques." For Mr. An, a second-generation zainichi Korean, the fact that among the people who lived here 1,400 years ago, there was a theory that the people of the Korean Peninsula called the area "Musashino" "ramie/苧," "seed," and "field" using weaving techniques, and that this was then transformed into "musashi" was a major influence on his later way of life and expression The fact that there was a theory that the word "no" was called "seed" (moshi) and then transformed into "musashi" must have had a great influence on An's later way of life and activities.

The origin of the word "Muzashi/无邪志" has been attributed to the Ainu people and other indigenous peoples in the ancient land of "Mujashi," and there are various theories as to its origin. For example, there is a theory that the word "Musashi" is derived from the Ainu word "mun chashi," meaning "peaceful castle," and another theory based on the topography that "there was a province called Musa/身狭, which was later divided into Musagami/身狭上 and Musashimo/身狭下, and became Sagami and Musashi." Folklorist Kunio Yanagida also offers a theory that the name "Musa" comes from "steaming thickets to make sashi, or slash-and-burn farmland," and that "mu" is "mu" for "steaming". There are many other theories, and it is likely that Mr. An named the title of his first collection of poems after the theory of "ramie field" as it was closer to his own existence based on these theories. This does not mean that he has chosen either "Musashi Field" or "Ramie Seed Field," but rather that he has made them coexist in abundance. Historically, the indigenous Ainu, Jomon, Yayoi, Yamato court authorities, and foreign settlers must have fused together through various conflicts, such as the "Musashinokuni no Miyakko" rebellion. Various theories have been written about the traces of the lives of the many people who cultivated "Musashino" and lived in harmony with nature.

2

The English-Japanese poetry collection "*MUSASHINO*/武蔵野" (translated by Noriko Mizusaki) by Toshiaki An has now been published. This bilingual English-Japanese poetry collection is a translation of his poetry collection "*MUSASHINO*" published in 2022, with the English text on the left of each page and the original Japanese text on the right. An enrolled in the English Literature Department of Sophia University, but later moved to the Philosophy Department and graduated from the Graduate School of Philosophy. He expressed to me his strong desire to have his collection of poems "Musashino" made into an English-Japanese poetry collection, "*MUSASHINO*/武蔵野," so that people around the world could read it. The beauty of An's poetry is condensed into words, and I anticipated difficulties in translating it, but Ms. Noriko Mizusaki, an English literature scholar and the actual author of poetry, tanka, and haiku, agreed to take on the task. In my opinion, her creativity, especially in the lyricism of tanka poetry, has been put to good use in the translation, resulting in an excellent translation that understands the spirit of Ms. An.

The English-Japanese poetry collection consists of 13 chapters: "Musashino" (Chapter 1), "Kashi no Yado" (Chapter 2), "Hiyodori" (Chapter 3), "Moment" (Chapter 4), "Pomegranate Flower" (Chapter 5), "Hosenka" (Chapter 6), "Fig Tree" (Chapter 7), "Kuko no Nuts" (Chapter 8), "Zanei" (Chapter 9), "Shizuku" (Chapter 10), "Mao-sa-shi-no : Field of Linen Grass" (Chapter 11), "Return" (Chapter 12), "Flower Shadow" (Chapter 12), and the final chapter "Hana no Shadow," along with An's prose poem, "*MUSASHINO*: On Destiny and Return."

The first four lines of "Chapter 1: Musashino" "武蔵野に／桑の実なる頃／君に／出会えり" are translated as "In Musashino / Around the time when / Mulberries ripen / I met / You." Mizusaki's translation of "ripen / 熟す" in the wilds of "Musashino" is very pleasant, and points to a naturalistic lyricism. At the same time, a fateful moment encounter with "you"in"Musashino" rises in the lines of poetry.

The two five lines "武蔵野の／楢紅葉／一葉は／君と僕の／しるし"are translated as "In Musashino / Oak leaf turned red / Each leaf is / The sign / Of you and me". "Oak leaf turned red" symbolizes the beauty of the autumn leaves of deciduous trees in "Musashino" in autumn. Why does the translator translate "One leaf" as "Each leaf" instead of "One leaf/ 一葉"? The translator probably translated "Each" to mean "one by one" to symbolize the many autumn leaves in "Musashino".The "leaf" is a "sign" of "you and me". It seems as if they are dreaming that their relationship will deepen and grow closer together, and that one day they will be returned to the nature of "Musashino" as beautifully as the oak maple leaves. If you read the poem thinking that it is a naturalistic lyric poem, you will be immediately betrayed. For example, in the fourth line of the fourth stanza, the two poets respect each other's independence, saying, "I am constantly / returning / to my true self," and then they return to "My true self" and calmly begin to explore how "you and I" should relate to each other. You will notice that the phrase "My true self/自己本来" is a psalm that contains Mr.An's ideological and philosophical speculation, in which he tries to live sincerely by asking the question of the meaning of existence, what is the true self?

The five lines of the fifth series, "その都度／時熟し／独り言のように／語

る” are translated as “Each time / When time ripens / I talk / Just to myself”. In these four lines, when the time ripens, Mr. An is probably mut-
tering to himself, prompting him to do something. The translation of “そ
の都度” as “Each time” may indicate that time is a series of disclosures of
the essential time as “time ripens. Mr. An studied mainly German philosophy at Sophia University. In “Being and Time” by the German philoso-
pher Heidegger, the phrase “zeitigen/時熟する” appears. It can also be
translated as “to temporalize” or “to ripen oneself as time” . Mr.An may
have used it in the poem as “tokijukushi” (時熟し), which is a reading of
the word in the Japanese language. This function is accompanied by a
determination, a “temporalization” to go beyond the non-native self of
the “present” from the “future” and become the “original self”. We come
to understand the theme of this full-length suite of poems as the determination and re-living of something called by the original being in the
encounter with a woman and a variety of plants in “Musashino.”

As we can read it, it becomes clear from the opening five stanzas that the
total of 59 stanzas in the chapter are contemplative psalms that are some-
times modulated and have an ontological perspective, although their
main investigation is lyric poetry. In “Musashino,” he encounters a
19-year-old woman who is like an incarnation of the muse, and the strug-
gle of middle-aged men with an age difference to live out their destiny of
needing each other, while harboring forbidden thoughts that they cannot
transgress, is described with a unique sense of rhythm.
The five lines of the 52nd sequence, “君と僕／転倒す／あらゆる価値／
再び／見出しつつ” are translated as “You and me / Tumble down / Finding out / All the values / Afresh”. One can imagine that the union of the
two men has caused a great deal of embarrassment to their families, and

has torn apart their existing relationships. "Tumble down/転倒する" means to tumble down the stairs, so they must have embarked on a new value, even preparing to risk their lives.

The final four lines of the final sequence, "運命の／許すものと／許さ ぬ／ものと" are translated as "My destiny / Permits some to me / Not does some to me". We are told that Mr. An became a Christian at the age of 19. As I read this last series, I can feel his fear that God may not be able to forgive him for his own acts. It seems as if God wants him to admit that there is something "forgivable" even if only a part of it.

3

The following are the important chapters from the second to the last chapter.

Chapter 2, "樫の宿" is translated as "Live Oak's Lodge." "楢" is translated as "oak" in the first chapter, but "樫" is translated as "live oak" in the second chapter. In the West, the distinction between oak and oak is ambiguous. In Japan, the difference is made clear by the fact that oak/楢 is deciduous and live oak/樫 is evergreen. It seems that Mr. An has entrusted a special meaning to the "live" in "live oak." Not content with graduate school lectures, Mr. An told me that he particularly studied and researched Dilthey's "philosophy of life" and Jaspers' existentialism in German philosophy, starting with Kant, by reading original texts with Czech professor Ludwig Armbruster. Dilthey said that in history, culture, and society, "will, emotion, and intellect" have a unified "structural linkage of life/生" and that all personal experience in such a world is "life/生" (Leben). He believes that such "life" objectifies diverse cultures such as language, law, religion, literature, and philosophy, and creates an "objective mode of life". We will attempt to examine and discuss the various "historical consciousness," "spirit of the times," "historical forms," and other worldviews. In reading "Musashino," An's long poem "Musashino," we cannot help but think that he is aiming for an "objective mode of life" in which "will, emotion, and intellect," with Dilthey's "historical consciousness," have a unified "structural relation of life" and attempt to describe the whole personal experience.

The 13th line of the second chapter, "金木犀／善悪の／彼岸／香りをり" is translated as "Fragrant olive blossoms / Beyond another shore / of right and wrong / Scenting" . It is likely that Mr. An took a hint from Nietzsche's "Beyond the Shore of Right and Wrong," Dilthey's "Structural Linkage of Life," and other philosophical speculations, and transformed them into the power of life to overcome the obstacles.

The next ten lines of the 14th series, "ひよ鳥／鳴いて／夏草／揺るゝ／樫の宿／君と僕／過去現在／未来と／接する／ところ" is translated as "A bulbul bird / Sings / Summer grass / Swaying / At the live oak's lodge / Where / For you and me / The past / The present / And the future / Adjoin together". The oak house is their abode filled with eternal greenery, and a bright future of hope seems to have faintly opened up from the painful past and present.

In chapter 3, "Bulbul Bird/むく鳥" the eight lines of the 45th stanza, "君を／愛することは／神に返すこと／自らの／罪に返すこと／無の愛に／目覚め／ゆくこと" are translated "To love / You is / To return it to God / To return it to my blames / My awakening to love / Requiring no gains". as It speaks of the ultimate love that is transparent: to love you is to return it to God, leading to the "love of nothing".

In chapter 4, "Moment / 一瞬", line 3 of the 42nd series, "樫の葉／樫の葉の雫／揺る" is translated as "Live oak leaves / Live oak leave's raindrops / Sway". Also, the fourth line of the 43rd series, "一雫／一瞬の／永遠" is translated as "The one drop / Eternity / In an instant". Mr.An finds eternity in the one drop on the oak leaf, as if each moment of living with a new woman feels like an eternity.

In subsequent chapters, he continues to praise the creatures as beings of equal value to his beloved "you", naming the indigenous names of the diverse creatures of "Musashino". These are: chapter 5 "Pomegranate Flowers/ざくろ花", chapter 6 "Balsam Flowers/鳳仙花", chapter 7 "Fig Tree", chapter 8 "Gojiberry/枸杞の実", chapter 9 "Remaining Shadow/残影", chapter 10 "Water Drops/雫", chapter 11 The titles of chapters 11, "Mao-sa-shi-no : Field of Linen Grass/苧種子野" and 12, "Return/回帰" are also clear.Rather, they are themselves kept alive by those diverse creatures, and the two "Kashi no Yado" make us glad to have a corner of them. We read that "Kimi" will become a Red Cross nurse, and that Mr. An will be there to support her as she deepens her career. In Mr. An's gaze, we can always sense the stern gaze of God entrusting "Kimi" to him, and it seems to me that this tension creates a consistent sense of rhythm in the grand suite of poems.

In the last section, "Flower Shadow," there is a confessional couplet as follows.

The fifth of the 53 stanzas, "With my wife / I walked / I parted from her

/ The sea / Shines," is translated as "With my wife / I walked / I parted from her / The sea / Shines". The woman recalls memories of walking along the shining seashore with her parted "wife," not the "you" she is now. It is evident that Mr. An has finally come to a place in his life where he is ready to accept all the memories of meeting and parting with his "wife".

Finally, I would like to quote the next 66 lines of the next and final chapter, which are etched in my mind.

These 13 lines, "すべてのことに／悲しみの声／聞こゆ／されど／また聞けば／すべてのことに／喜びの声／聞こえ来る／神我に／すべてのことを／与えけり／悲しみと／喜びの声なり"are translated as"On all daily affairs / Voices of sorrow / I hear / Though / I listen to them again / On all these things / Voices of joy / I can hear / God / Gave me / All / Voices of / Sorrows and Joys". Mr.An was strongly influenced by Dilthey's "philosophy of life" mentioned earlier as well as by the "inclusivist" existential philosophy of Jaspers. According to Jaspers, "existence" is something that can never be objectified, and it is a matter of remembering, awakening, and living out what one is. In doing so, he believes it is necessary to be supported by God, the transcendent. Jaspers refers to the transcendent God as "the Inclusive One," and he makes Him the basis for the salvation of existence in extreme situations. The "God" in Mr.An's line, "God give me / all things…" may refer to the function of the "Inclusor" in Jaspers. In the extreme situation of receiving the voice of sorrow and the voice of joy at the same time, Mr. An must continue to perceive "God" through the "Inclusor". Like Kierkegaard's spirit of "repetition," Mr. An has continued to question his hometown of "Musashino" and has finally

created an English-Japanese poetry collection, "*MUSASHINO*/武蔵野".
I sincerely hope that this collection of English-Japanese poems will be
read and passed on to people in Japan, Korea and other Asian countries,
as well as to people around the world who will create an old village where
diversity can be respected and coexist in harmony.

解説

古里「武蔵野」を奏でる三千行もの抒情・存在論的な思索詩

安俊暉英日詩集『*MUSASHINO*／武蔵野』（水崎野里子訳）に寄せて

鈴木比佐雄

1

　安俊暉氏の「武蔵野」詩篇は、1連3〜7行の短詩中心の詩行が組詩として積み重ねられていく。読み始めると今ここの意識の流れのリズム感に引き込まれていく。そしていつの間にか「武蔵野」に生かされる男女と数多の植物や小鳥たちが立ち現れてくるイメージが喚起し、既視感のような私たちの記憶の深層や古層に気付かされてしまう。そして安氏の古層と私たちの深層がどこかつながっていく不可思議で豊饒な体験を感ずることになる。安氏の詩篇は、忘れていた深層や古層に向けて遡るような思いを懐かせて、私たちの内面のしなやかな感受性に呼応し、かつて私たちの多様な先祖が息づいて活動していた古里「武蔵野」の記憶を、あたかもバッハの無伴奏チェロ組曲のように三千行もの組詩として奏でられている。と同時にその背後には叙情詩でありながら、存在論的な問いを発した生々しい思索が詩の中に宿っている。

　「武蔵野」は「武蔵」の野原ということだ。その「武蔵」が初めて歴史書上に記されたのは、530年代に「武蔵 国 造 の乱」として日本書紀に登場した。当時は「无邪志」（むざし）とも言われていたらしく、後の七世紀に「武蔵」（むさし）という漢字の地域名に統一されて公的に記されたようだ。「国造」とは「大化の改新以前における世襲制の地方官」のことだが、どれほどの権限があったかは謎の部分も多い。その地の歴史に、豪族の内紛に大和朝廷が介入する「乱」があったのだ。その地域は多摩川から荒川にまたがる神奈川、東京、埼玉の関東平野の中心部分を指し示していたと言われている。その「武

蔵野」に由来する「武蔵野線」は、私の暮らす千葉県から始まり埼玉県を経て都下の府中まで、かつては原野が続いていたが、今は郊外のベッドタウンを貫き、東京の中心を取り囲むように走り続けている。

その「武蔵野」に紀元6世紀前後に朝鮮半島から数多くの渡来人が様々な技術を持って到来してきたのだろう。現在の都下の「狛江」や「埼玉県高麗郡」などには、高句麗の人びとの記憶が刻まれている。その記憶の中から呼ばれるように安氏は2002年に第一詩集『苧種子野（むさしの）』を刊行し、2005年に詩集『桑の実』を刊行した。その2冊を基にして20年後の2022年に詩集『武蔵野』（日本語版）を刊行した。本質的な詩人は生涯に唯一の詩集を残すために生きるとも言われている。安氏もこの詩集『武蔵野』を残すために生きてこられたように感じさせてくれる。安氏は詩集『苧種子野（むさしの）』のあとがきで、「ある研究書によると、武蔵野の語源が朝鮮語であり、織物の技術と共に持ち来たった麻の一種、「苧（からむし）の野」という意味によるものとあった」と記している。在日朝鮮人二世の安氏にとって、1400年前からこの地で生きた人びとの中に、朝鮮半島の人びとが織物の技術を生かして、「武蔵野」の地を「苧」（モシ）「種子」（シ）「野」（の）と呼んでいて、それが「ムサシ」に転化していった説があったことは、その後の安氏の生き方や表現活動に大きな影響を与えたのだろう。

因みに古代の「无邪志」（むざし）と言われていた土地において、その古層には先住民のアイヌ人などとの様々な関係でその語源も様々な説が存在している。例えば『ムサシは、平和な城を意味するアイヌ語「ムン・チャシ」に由来する』という説や、また国学者の賀茂真淵は「身狭（ムサ）国があり、後に身狭上（ムサガミ）と身狭下（ムサシモ）に分かれて相模と武蔵となった」という地形的な説を唱えた。また民俗学者の柳田国男は「雑木林を蒸（ム）して焼畑農地（サシ）を作るに由来し、「ム」は蒸すのムである」との暮らしからの説を

語っている。その他にも数多くの説があり、安氏はそれらの説を踏まえて、「苧（からむし）の野」の説が自らの存在に近いものとして第一詩集のタイトルに名付けたのだろう。それは「武蔵野」と「苧種子野」のどちらかを選ぶというわけではなく、それらを豊かに共存させてきたということだろう。歴史的にも先住民のアイヌ人や縄文人、また弥生人、大和朝廷の権力者たち、渡来人たちが「武蔵国 造 の乱」などの様々な軋轢を経て、いつしか融合し合っていったのだろう。そして「武蔵野」を開拓して自然との共生を図ってきた数多の人びとの暮らしの痕跡が様々な説の中に記憶されている。

　　　2
　今回、安俊暉英日詩集『*MUSASHINO*／武蔵野』（水崎野里子訳）が刊行された。本詩集は、2022年に刊行した詩集『武蔵野』を翻訳し、一頁の左に英文を、右に日本語の原文を配置した対訳の英日詩集である。安氏は上智大学の英文科に入学したが、後に哲学科に移り哲学研究科大学院を卒業している。安氏は詩集『武蔵野』を英日詩集『*MUSASHINO*／武蔵野』にして世界の人びとに読んでもらいたいという強い願いを私に語ってくれた。安氏の詩篇は凝縮された言葉の美であり、翻訳をすることは困難が予想されたが、英文学者で詩、短歌、俳句の実作者である水崎野里子氏が引き受けてくれた。特に短歌の抒情性を生かした創作力が翻訳にも生かされていて、安氏の精神を理解した優れた翻訳になっていると私は考えている。
　英日詩集は、一章「武蔵野」、二章「樫の宿」、三章「ひよ鳥」、四章「一瞬」、五章「ざくろ花」、六章「鳳仙花」、七章「無花果」、八章「枸杞の実」、九章「残影」、十章「雫」、十一章「苧種子野」、十二章「回帰」、終章「花の影」の十三章と安氏の散文「詩集『武蔵野』運命と回帰」から成り立っている。
　「一章　武蔵野」の1連目の4行「武蔵野に／桑の実なる頃／君に／

出会えり」は、「In Musashino / Around the time when / Mulberries ripen / I met / You」と訳されている。この「武蔵野」の原野で「ripen ／熟す」という水崎氏の訳がとても心地よく、自然主義的な抒情性を指し示している。と同時に「君」との「武蔵野」での出会いに運命的な瞬間が立ち上がってくる。

2連の5行「武蔵野の／楢紅葉／一葉は／君と僕の／しるし」は「In Musashino / Oak leaf turned red / Each leaf is / The sign / Of you and me」と訳されている。「楢紅葉」を「Oak leaf turned red」として秋の「武蔵野」の落葉樹の紅葉の美しさを象徴させている。その「一葉」を「One leaf」ではなく「Each leaf」と訳しているのはなぜだろうか。翻訳者は「Each」には「一つひとつ」の意味があり、「一葉」に「武蔵野」の数多の紅葉を象徴させるためにそのように訳したのだろう。その「一つひとつ」の「一葉」が「君と僕の／しるし」であるとは、二人の関係が深まり寄り添って、いつか楢紅葉のように美しく「武蔵野」の自然に還元してゆくことを夢想しているかのようだ。

このように自然主義的な抒情詩だと思い読み進めていくと、その思いは直ぐに裏切られてしまう。例えば4連目の4行「絶えず／自己本来に／たち帰り／居る」と互いの自立を尊重し合い、さらに「自己本来／My true self」に立ち帰り冷静になって「君と僕」の互いの関係の在り方を探り始めていく。この「自己本来／My true self」という言葉は、本来的な自己とは何かという存在の意味の問いを発して、誠実に生きようとする安氏の思想・哲学的な思索を宿した詩篇だと気付くだろう。

5連の5行「その都度／時熟し／独り言のように／語る」は「Each time / When time ripens / I talk / Just to myself」と訳されている。この4行は、時が熟したと安氏が呟いて何かを促されるのだろう。「その都度」を「Each time」と訳したのは、時間が「時が熟す」ような本来的な時間が開示する連続であることを示しているのだろう。安氏は上

213

智大学で主にドイツ哲学を学んだ。ドイツの哲学者のハイデガーの『存在と時間』の中に『時熟する／zeitigen』という言葉が出てくる。「時間化する」とか「自らを時間として熟させる」とも訳される。安氏はそれを「時熟し（ときじゅくし）」として詩の中でしなやかに訓読みで使用したのだろう。この働きは「将来」から「現在」の非本来的な自己を超えて、「自己本来」になろうとする「時間化」である決意性を伴っている。「武蔵野」の中で一人の女性や多様な植物との出会いの中で、本来的な存在に呼ばれて何かを決意し生き直していくことがこの長編組詩のテーマであると私たちに理解されてくる。

　このように読み取れるように、一章の計59連の詩篇は、主な調べは抒情詩でありながらも、時に転調して存在論的な視座をもつ思索的な詩篇であることが冒頭の5連からも明らかになってくる。「武蔵野」の中でミューズの化身のような19歳の女性と出会い、年齢差のある中年の男性が踏み越えていけない禁忌な思いを懐きつつ、それでも互いを必要とする宿命を生きようとする格闘が、独特なリズム感となって記されている。

　52連の5行「君と僕／転倒す／あらゆる価値／再び／見出しつつ」は、「You and me / Tumble down / Finding out / All the values / Afresh」と訳されている。二人が結ばれたことは、二人の家族たちを困惑させて、大変な事態を引き起こし、今までの人間関係を切り裂いてしまったことは想像される。「転倒する／Tumble down」とは、階段から転がり落ちるという意味なので、命の危機さえ覚悟しながら、新たな価値に踏み出したのだろう。

　最終連の4行「運命の／許すものと／許さぬ／ものと」は「My destiny / Permits some to me / Not does some to me」と訳されている。安氏は19歳でクリスチャンになったと聞いている。この最終連を読む限り、自己の行為を神は許すことができないのではないかという恐れおののきが伝わってくる。その中にも神は一部だけでも「許すもの」

があると認めて欲しいと願っているかのようだ。

　　　3
　二章から最終章までの重要な連を次にあげていきたい。
　二章「樫の宿」は「Live Oak's Lodge」と訳されている。一章に出
てきた楢が「oak」と訳されているが、樫は「live oak」と訳し分けら
れている。欧米では楢と樫の区別は曖昧であり、両方とも「oak」で
あったらしい。日本では楢が落葉樹であり、樫が常緑樹であることか
らその違いを明らかにしている。この樫の「live oak」の「live」に安
氏は特別な意味を託しているように思われる。大学院の講義に飽き足
らず、チェコ人のルートヴィヒ・アルムブルスター教授との原書講読
などで特に学び研究したのが、カントを起点としたドイツ哲学のディ
ルタイの「生の哲学」やヤスパースの実存主義だと安氏から聞いてい
る。ディルタイは、歴史や文化や社会の中で「意志、感情、知性」
が、統一的な「生の構造連関」を持っていて、そこでの全ての人間的
体験が「生」（Leben）であるという。そのような「生」は言語・法
律・宗教・文学・哲学などの多様な文化を客観化し、「生の客観態」
を生み出すと考える。その様々な「歴史意識」、「時代精神」、「歴史的
形態」などの世界観を検証し考察しようと試みる。安氏の「武蔵野」
を読んでいると、ディルタイの「歴史意識」を持ち、「意志、感情、
知性」が、統一的な「生の構造連関」を持ち、全人間的な体験を記そ
うとする「生の客観態」を長編詩で目指しているのだと思われてなら
ない。
　二章の13連の4行「金木犀／善悪の／彼岸／香りをり」は、
「Fragrant olive blossoms ／ Beyond another shore ／ of right and wrong ／
Scenting」と訳されている。きっとニーチェの、「善悪の彼岸」や、
ディルタイの「生の構造連関」などの哲学的な思索力をヒントにし、
安氏は生きる力に転換して乗り越えていったのだろう。

次の14連の10行「ひよ鳥／鳴いて／夏草／揺る丶／樫の宿／君と僕／過去現在／未来と／接する／ところ」は、「A bulbul bird / Sings / Summer grass / Swaying / At the live oak's lodge / Where / For you and me / The past / The present / And the future / Adjoin together」と訳されている。樫の家は永遠の緑に満ちた二人の住まいであり、苦しかった過去・現在から明るい希望の未来がかすかに開かれてきたのだろう。

　三章「むく鳥／Bulbul Bird」の45連の8行「君を／愛することは／神に返すこと／自らの／罪に返すこと／無の愛に／目覚め／ゆくこと」は、「To love / You is / To return it to God / To return it to my blames / My awakening to love / Requiring no gains」と訳されている。君を愛することが、神に返すことであり、「無の愛」に至るという透徹した究極の愛を物語っている。

　四章「一瞬／Moment」の42連の3行「樫の葉／樫の葉の雫／揺る丶」と43連の4行「一雫／一瞬の／永遠」は、「Live oak leaves / Live oak leaves' raindrops / Sway」、「The one drop / Eternity / In an instant」と訳されている。安氏は新しき女性と暮らす一瞬一瞬を永遠に感じるように、樫の葉に付いた一雫に永遠を見出している。

　その後の章では、五章「ざくろ花／Pomegranate Flowers」、六章「鳳仙花／Balsam Flowers」、七章「無花果／Fig Tree」、八章「枸杞の実／Gojiberry」、九章「残影／Remaining Shadow」、十章「雫／Water Drops」、十一章「苧種子野／Mao-sa-shi-no：Field of Linen Grass」、十二章「回帰／Return」のタイトルでも明らかなように「武蔵野」の多様な生き物の固有名を挙げながら、愛する「君」と同等の価値を有する存在者として、生き物たちを讃美し続けている。むしろその多様な生き物たちから自分たちが生かされていて、二人の「樫の宿」はそ

の一隅を得ていることに喜びを感じさせてくれる。「君」は赤十字の看護師となり、そのキャリアを深めていくことを安氏が支えていく存在になることが読み取れる。その安氏の視線にはいつも神からの「君」を託された厳しい眼差しが感じられて、その緊張感が壮大な組詩に一貫したリズム感を生み出しているように私には感じられる。

　最後の終章「花の影／FLOWER SHADOW」では、次のような告白的な連がある。

　53連の5行「妻と／歩き／別れし／海／光る」は、「With my wife / I walked / I parted from her / The sea / Shines」と訳されている。女性は今の「君」ではなく、別れた「妻」と輝く海辺を歩いた思い出が回想されている。安氏はようやく、「妻」との出会いから別れるまでの思い出の全てを受け入れる心境になってきたことがうかがえる。

　最後に私の中で心に刻まれる次の最終章の66連を引用したい。

　この13行「すべてのことに／悲しみの声／聞こゆ／されど／また聞けば／すべてのことに／喜びの声／聞こえ来る／神我に／すべてのことを／与えけり／悲しみと／喜びの声なり」は、「On all daily affairs / Voices of sorrow / I hear / Though / I listen to them again / On all these things / Voices of joy / I can hear / God / Gave me / All / Voices of / Sorrows and Joys」と訳されている。安氏は先に触れたディルタイの「生の哲学」と同時にヤスパースの実存哲学の「包括者」からも強い影響を受けた。ヤスパースは「実存」が決して客観視することができないもので、自分自身が何であるかを想起し目覚めさせそれを生きることだという。その際に超越者である神から支持される必要があると考える。ヤスパースは超越者である神を「包括者」と言い、極限情況の実存を救済する拠り所にする。安氏の詩行の「神我に／すべてのことを／与えけり」に出てくる「神」とは、ヤスパースの「包括者」の働きを指し示しているだろう。「悲しみの声」と「喜びの声」を同時に受け止

める極限状況において、安氏はその「包括者」を介して「神」を感受
し続けているのだろう。安氏はキルケゴールの「反復」の精神のよう
に「武蔵野」という古里を問い続けて、ついには英日詩集
『*MUSASHINO*／武蔵野』を創造してしまった。この英日詩集が日本
を越えて、韓国などのアジア、さらに世界中の多様性を尊重されて共
生できる古里を創造していく人びとに、読み継がれることを心から
願っている。

著者略歴

安　俊暉（あん　としあき）

1943年、茨城県に、在日韓国人として生れる。
上智大学大学院哲学研究科修了。

［著書］
詩集『苧種子野』（思潮社）、詩集『桑の実』（思潮社）

Biography of The Author

Toshiaki An

Born 1943, in Ibaraki Prefecture, to a Japanese Korean resident in
Japan.

He finished the Graduate School of Sophia University. He Studied
Philosophy.

[Books]

Collected Poems of Toshiaki An, *Maosashino: A Field of Linen Grass.*

(Published by Shichosya, in Tokyo).

Collected Poems of Toshiaki An, *Mulberries.*

(Published by Shichosya)

住所

〒 981-3203
　宮城県仙台市泉区高森 6-1-1 2-105

E-mail : toshi.an@yahoo.co.uk

訳者紹介

水崎　野里子（みずさき　のりこ）

1949年、東京都武蔵野市吉祥寺に生れる。
早稲田大学大学院英米文学科修了。

［翻訳書・著書］
ディヴィッド・クリーガー詩集『神の涙─広島・長崎原爆　国
境を越えて』（翻訳）（コールサック社）
歌集『全山紅葉』（コールサック社）

Biography of The Translator

Noriko Mizusaki

Born 1949, in Kichijoji, Musashino-shi, Tokyo.

She finished the Graduate Course of Waseda University. She Studied
English and American Literature.

[Books]

As Translator:David Krieger *God's Tears--Reflections on the Atomic
Bombs Dropped on Hiroshima & Nagasaki.*

(Coal Sack Publishing Company)

As Poet: Collected Tanka Poem of Noriko Mizusaki, *Colored Leaves All
Over the Mountain.*

(Coal Sack Publishing Company)

石炭袋

The Collected Poems of Toshiaki An in English & Japanese
MUSASHINO ／英日詩集 武蔵野

2024 年 5 月 17 日初版発行
著者　　　　　安俊暉 /Toshiaki An
英文翻訳者　水崎野里子 /Noriko Mizusaki
編集・発行者　鈴木比佐雄 /Hisao Suzuki
発行所　株式会社 コールサック社
〒 173-0004　東京都板橋区板橋 2-63-4-209
電話 03-5944-3258　FAX 03-5944-3238
suzuki@coal-sack.com　http://www.coal-sack.com
郵便振替　00180-4-741802
印刷管理　（株）コールサック社　制作部

装幀　松本菜央

落丁本・乱丁本はお取り替えいたします。
ISBN978-4-86435-609-1　C0092　￥2300E

MUSASHINO

Coal Sack Publishing Company
2-63-4-209 Itabashi Itabashi-ku Tokyo 173-0004 Japan
Tel: (03)5944-3258 / Fax: (03)5944-3238
suzuki@coal-sack.com　http://www.coal-sack.com
President: Hisao Suzuki